Pratchett, Terry
Wings; the last book of the Bromeliad. Delacorte Press, 1991.
200 p.

I. Title.

WINGS

WINGS

The Last Book
of the Bromeliad

TERRY PRATCHETT

j
c.2

Delacorte Press

91

Published by
Delacorte Press
Bantam Doubleday Dell Publishing Group, Inc.
666 Fifth Avenue
New York, New York 10103

This work was originally published in Great
Britain by Transworld Publishers Ltd.

Library of Congress Cataloging in Publication Data

Pratchett, Terry.
    Wings/Terry Pratchett.
        p.   cm.
    Summary: Masklin, one of a race of beings four
inches high who live secretly among humans, tries to
use the portable computer known as Thing to summon back the spaceship in which his ancestors came
to Earth.
    ISBN 0-385-30436-6
    [1. Science fiction.]   I. Title.
PZ7.P8865Wi   1991   90-48457
[Fic]—dc20   CIP
                                             AC

Manufactured in the United States of America

October 1991

10 9 8 7 6 5 4 3 2 1

BVG

To Lyn and Rhianna
and the
sandwich-eating alligator
at the Kennedy Space Center,
Cape Canaveral, Florida

Author's note: No character in this book is intended to resemble any living creature of whatever size on any continent, especially if they've got lawyers.

I've also taken liberties with the Concorde itself, despite British Airways's kindness in letting me have a look around one. It really does look like shaped sky. But it doesn't fly nonstop to Miami; it makes a stop in Washington. But who wants to stop in Washington? Nomes couldn't do anything in Washington except cause trouble.

It's also just possible that people on the Concorde don't have to eat the special airline-food pink wobbly stuff. But everybody else has to.

In the beginning . . .

. . . was Arnold Bros. (est. 1905), the great department store.

It was the home of several thousand nomes—as they called themselves—who'd long ago given up life in the countryside and settled down under the floorboards of Mankind.

Not that they had anything to do with humans. Humans were big and slow and stupid.

Nomes live fast. To them, ten years is like a century. Since they'd been living in the Store for more than eighty years, they'd long ago forgotten that there were things like Sun and Rain and Wind. All there was, was the Store—created by the legendary Arnold Bros. (est. 1905) as a proper place for nomes to live.

And then, into the Store from an Outside the nomes didn't believe existed, came Masklin and his little tribe. They knew what Rain and Wind were, all right. That's why they'd tried to get away from them.

With them they brought the Thing. For years they had thought of the Thing as a sort of talisman or lucky charm. Only in the Store, near electricity, did it wake up and tell a few selected nomes things they hardly understood.

They learned that they had originally come from the stars, in some sort of Ship, and that somewhere up in the sky that Ship had been waiting for thousands of years to take them home.

And they learned that the Store was going to be demolished in three weeks.

How Masklin tricked, bullied, and persuaded the nomes into leaving the Store by stealing one of its huge trucks is recounted in *Truckers*.

They made it to an old quarry, and for a little while things went well enough.

But when you're four inches high in a world full of giant people, things never go very well for very long.

They found that humans were going to reopen the quarry.

At the same time, they also found a scrap of newspaper that had a picture of Richard Arnold, grandson of one of the brothers who founded Arnold Bros. The company that had owned the Store was now a big international concern, and Grandson Richard, 39—said the newspaper—was going to Florida to watch the launch of its first communications satellite.

The Thing admitted to Masklin that, if it could get into space, it could call the Ship. He decided to take a few nomes and go to the airport and find some way of getting to Florida to get the Thing into the sky—which, of course, was ridiculous, as well as impossible. But he didn't know this, so he tried to do it anyway.

So, thinking that Florida was five miles away and possibly a kind of orange juice *anyway*,* and that there were perhaps several hundred human beings in the world, and not knowing where exactly to go or what to do when they got there, but determined to get there and do it *anyway*, Masklin and his companions set out.

The nomes that stayed behind fought the humans in *Diggers*. They defended their quarry as long as they could and fled on the Cat, the great yellow digging machine.

But this is Masklin's story. . . .

* The only time the nomes had seen the word "Florida" before was on an old carton of orange juice. When nomes get hold of an idea, they don't let go without a struggle.

One

Airports: A place where people hurry up and wait.
—From *A Scientific Encyclopedia for the Enquiring Young Nome* by Angalo de Haberdasheri.

Let the eye of your imagination be a camera. . . .

This is the universe, a glittering ball of galaxies like the ornament on some unimaginable Christmas tree.

Find a galaxy. . . . *Focus.*

This is a galaxy, swirled like the cream in a cup of coffee, every pinpoint of light a star.

Find a star. . . . *Focus.*

This is a solar system, where planets barrel through the darkness around the central fires of the sun. Some planets hug close, hot enough to melt lead. Some drift far out, where the comets are born.

Find a blue planet. . . . *Focus.*

This is a planet. Most of it is covered in water. It's called Earth.

Find a country. . . . *Focus.* . . . Blues and greens and browns under the sun, and here's a pale oblong, which is . . . *focus* . . . an airport, a concrete hive for silver bees. There's a . . . *focus* . . . building full of people and noise, and . . . *focus* . . . a hall of lights and bustle, and . . . *focus* . . . a bin full of rubbish, and . . . *focus* . . . a pair of tiny eyes. . . .

Focus. . . . *Focus.* . . . *Focus.* . . . Click!

Masklin slid cautiously down an old burger carton.

He'd been watching humans. Hundreds and hundreds of humans. It was beginning to dawn on him that getting on a jet plane wasn't like stealing a truck.

Angalo and Gurder had nestled deep into the rubbish and were gloomily eating the remains of a cold, greasy french fry.

This has come as a shock to all of us, Masklin thought.

I mean, take Gurder. Back in the Store he was the Abbot. He believed that Arnold Bros. made the Store for nomes. And he still thinks there's some sort of Arnold Bros. somewhere, watching over us, because we were important. And now we're out here and all we've found is that nomes aren't important at all. . . .

And there's Angalo. He doesn't believe in Arnold Bros., but he likes to think Arnold Bros. exists just so that he can go on not believing in him.

And there's me.

I never thought it would be this hard.

I thought jet planes were just trucks with more wings and less wheels.

There's more humans in this place than I've ever seen before. How can we find Grandson Richard, 39, in a place like this?

I hope they're going to save me some of that french fry.

Angalo looked up.

"Seen him?" he said, sarcastically.

Masklin shrugged. "There are lots of humans with beards," he said. "They all look the same to me."

"I *told* you," said Angalo. "Blind faith never works." He glared at Gurder.

"He could have gone already," said Masklin. "He could have walked right past me."

"So let's get back," said Angalo. "People will be missing us. We've made the effort, we've seen the airport, we've nearly got stepped on *dozens* of times. Now let's get back to the real world."

"What do you think, Gurder?" said Masklin.

The Abbot gave him a long, despairing look.

"I don't know," he said. "I really don't know. I'd hoped . . ."

His voice trailed off. He looked so downcast that even Angalo patted him on the shoulder.

"Don't take it so hard," he said. "You didn't *really* think some sort of Grandson Richard, 39, was going to swoop down out of the sky and carry us off to Florida, did you? Look, we've given it a try. It hasn't worked. Let's go home."

"Of course I didn't think *that,*" said Gurder irritably. "I just thought that . . . maybe in some way . . . there'd be a way."

"The world belongs to humans. They built everything. They run everything. We might as well accept it," said Angalo.

Masklin looked at the Thing. He knew it was listening. Even though it was just a small black cube, it somehow always looked more alert when it was listening.

The trouble was, it only spoke when it felt like it. It'd always give you just enough help, and no more. It seemed to be testing him the whole time.

Somehow, asking the Thing for help was like admitting that you'd run out of ideas. But . . .

"Thing," he said, "I know you can hear me, because there must be loads of electricity in this building. We're at the airport. We can't find Grandson Richard, 39. We don't know how to *start* looking. Please help us."

The Thing stayed silent.

"If you *don't* help us," said Masklin quietly, "we'll go back to the quarry and face the humans, but that won't matter to you because we'll leave you here. We really will. And no nomes will ever find you again. There will never be another chance. We'll die out, there will be no more nomes anywhere, and it will be because of you. And in years and years to come you'll be all alone and useless and you'll think 'Perhaps I should have helped Masklin when he asked me,' and then you'll think 'If I had my time all over again, I *would* have helped him.' Well, Thing, imagine all that has happened and you've magically got your wish. Help us."

"It's a machine!" snapped Angalo. "You can't blackmail a machine—!"

One small red light lit up on the Thing's black surface.

"I know you can tell what other machines are thinking," said Masklin. "But can you tell what nomes are thinking? Read my mind, Thing, if you don't think I'm serious. You want nomes to act intelligently. Well, I *am* acting intelligently. I'm intelligent enough to know when I need help. I need help now. And you can help. I know you can. If you don't help us now, we'll leave right now and forget you ever existed."

A second light came on, very faintly.

Masklin stood up, and nodded to the other.

"All right," he said. "Let's go."

The Thing made a little electronic noise, which

was the machine's equivalent of a nome clearing his throat.

"How can I be of assistance?" it said.

Angalo grinned at Gurder.

Masklin sat down again.

"Find Grandson Richard Arnold, 39," he said.

"This will take a long time," said the Thing.

"Oh."

A few lights moved on the Thing's surface. Then it said, *"I have located a Richard Arnold, aged 39. He has just gone into the departure lounge for Flight 205 to Miami, Florida."*

"That didn't take a very long time," said Masklin.

"It was three hundred microseconds," said the Thing. *"That's long."*

"I don't think I understood all of it too," Masklin added.

"Which parts didn't you understand?"

"Nearly all of them," said Masklin. "All the bits after 'gone into.' "

"Someone with the right name is here and waiting in a special room to get on a big silver bird that flies in the sky to go to a place called Florida," said the Thing.

"What big silver bird?" said Angalo.

"It means jet plane. It's being sarcastic," said Masklin.

"Yeah? How does it know all this stuff?" said Angalo, suspiciously.

"This building is full of computers," said the Thing.

"What, like you?"

The Thing managed to look offended. *"They are very, very primitive,"* it said. *"But I can understand them. If I think slowly enough. Their job is to know where humans are going."*

"That's more than most humans do," said Angalo.

"Can you find out how we can get to him?" said Gurder, his face alight.

"Hold on, hold on," said Angalo, quickly. "Let's not rush into things here."

"We came here to find him, didn't we?" said Gurder.

"Yes! But what do we actually *do*?"

"Well, of course, we . . . we . . . that is, we'll . . ."

"We don't even know what a departure lounge is."

"The Thing said it's a room where humans wait to get on an airplane," said Masklin.

Gurder prodded Angalo with an accusing finger.

"You're frightened, aren't you?" he said. "You're frightened that if we see Grandson Richard, 39, it'll mean there really *is* an Arnold Bros. and you'll have been *wrong*! You're just like your father. He could never stand being wrong, either!"

"I'm frightened about *you*," said Angalo. "Because you'll see that Grandson Richard, 39, is just a human. Arnold Bros. was just a human too. Or two humans. They just built the Store for humans. They didn't even know about nomes! And you can leave my father out of this too."

The Thing opened a small hatch on its top. It did that sometimes. When the hatches were shut you couldn't see where they were, but whenever the Thing was really interested in something it opened up and extended a small silver dish on a pole, or a complicated arrangement of pipes.

This time it was a piece of wire mesh on a metal rod. It started to turn, slowly.

Masklin picked it up.

While the other two argued he said, quietly, "Do you know where this lounge thing is?"

"*Yes,*" said the Thing.

"Let's go, then."

Angalo looked around.

"Hey, what are you doing?" he said.

Masklin ignored him. He said to the Thing, "And do you know how much time we have before he starts going to Florida?"

"*About half an hour.*"

Nomes live ten times faster than humans. They're harder to see than a high-speed mouse.

That's one reason why most humans hardly ever see them.

The other is that humans are very good at not seeing things they know aren't there. And since sensible humans know that there are no such things as four-inch-high people, a nome who doesn't want to be seen probably *won't* be seen.

So no one noticed three tiny blurs darting across the floor of the airport building. They dodged the rumbling wheels of luggage carts. They shot between the legs of slow-moving humans. They skidded around chairs. They became nearly invisible as they crossed a huge, echoing corridor.

And they disappeared behind a potted plant.

It has been said that everything everywhere affects everything else. This may be true.

Or perhaps the world is just full of patterns.

For example, in a tree nine thousand miles away from Masklin, high on a cloudy mountainside, was a plant that looked like one large flower. It grew wedged in a fork of trees, its roots dangling in the air to trap what nourishment they could from the mists. Technically, it was an epiphytic bromeliad, although not knowing this made very little difference to the plant.

Water condensed into a tiny pool in the center of the bloom.

And there were frogs living in it.

Very, very small frogs.

They had such a tiny life cycle, it still had training wheels on it.

They hunted insects among the petals. They laid their eggs in the central pool. Tadpoles grew up and became more frogs. And they made more tadpoles. And each eventually died, and sank down and joined the compost at the base of the leaves, which, in fact, helped nourish the plant.

And this had been the way things were for as far back as the frogs could remember.*

Except that on this day, while it hunted for flies, one frog lost its way and crawled around the side of one of the outermost petals, or possibly leaves, and saw something it had never seen before.

It saw the universe.

More precisely, it saw the branch stretching away into the mists.

And several yards away, glistening with droplets of moisture in a solitary shaft of sunlight, was another flower.

The frog sat and stared.

"Hngh! Hngh! Hngh!"

Gurder leaned against the wall and panted like a hot dog on a sunny day.

Angalo was almost as badly out of breath, but was going red in the face trying not to show it.

"Why didn't you *tell* us!" he demanded.

"You were too busy arguing," said Masklin. "So I knew the only way to get you running was to start moving."

---

* About three seconds. Frogs don't have good memories.

"Thank . . . you . . . very much," Gurder heaved.

"Why aren't you puffed out?" said Angalo.

"I'm used to running fast," said Masklin, peering around the plant. "Okay, Thing. Now what?"

"Along this corridor," said the Thing.

"It's full of humans!" squeaked Gurder.

"Everywhere's full of humans. That's why we're doing this," said Masklin. He paused, and then added, "Look, Thing, isn't there any other way we can go? Gurder nearly got squashed just now."

Colored lights moved in complicated patterns across the Thing. Then it said, *"What is it you want to achieve?"*

"We must find Grandson Richard, 39," panted Gurder.

"No. Going to the Florida place is the important thing," said Masklin.

"It isn't!" said Gurder. "I don't want to go to any Florida!"

Masklin hesitated. Then he said, "This probably isn't the right time to say this, but I haven't been totally honest with you."

He told them about the Thing, and space, and the Ship in the sky. Around them there was the endless thundering noise of a building full of busy humans.

Eventually Gurder said, "You're not trying to find Grandson Richard, 39, at all?"

"I think he's probably very important," said Masklin hurriedly. "But you're right. At Florida there's a place where they have a sort of jet plane that goes straight up, to put kind of bleeping radio things in the sky."

"Oh, come *on*," said Angalo. "You can't just put things in the sky! They'd fall down."

"I don't really understand it myself," Masklin admitted. "But if you go up high enough, there is *no* down. I think. Anyway, all we have to do is go to Florida and put the Thing on one of these going-up jets and it can do the rest, it says."

"All?" said Angalo.

"It can't be harder than stealing a truck," said Masklin.

"You're not suggesting we *steal* a plane?" said Gurder, by this time totally horrified.

"Wow!" said Angalo, his eyes lighting up as if by some internal power source. He loved vehicles of all sorts—especially when they were traveling fast.

"You would, too, wouldn't you?" said Gurder accusingly.

"Wow!" said Angalo again. He seemed to be looking at a picture only he could see.

"You're mad," said Gurder.

"No one said anything about stealing a plane," said Masklin quickly. "We aren't going to steal a plane. We're just going for a ride on one, I hope."

"Wow!"

"And we're *not* going to try to drive it, Angalo!"

Angalo shrugged.

"All right," he said. "But suppose I'm on it, and the driver becomes ill, then I expect I'll have to take over. I mean, I drove the Truck pretty well—"

"You kept running *into* things!" said Gurder.

"I was learning. Anyway, there's nothing to run into in the sky except clouds, and they look pretty soft," said Angalo.

"There's the *ground*!"

"Oh, the ground wouldn't be a problem. It'd be too far away."

Masklin tapped the Thing. "Do you know where the jet plane is that's going to Florida?"

"*Yes.*"

"Lead us there, then. Avoiding as many humans as you can."

"And where does the orange juice come into all this?" said Gurder.

"I'm not too sure about the orange juice bit," said Masklin.

It was raining softly, and because it was early evening, lights were coming on around the airport.

Absolutely no one heard the faint tinkle as a little ventilation grille dropped off an outside wall.

Three blurred shapes lowered themselves down

onto the concrete and sped away, toward the planes.

Angalo looked up. And up some more. And there was still more up to come. He ended up with his head craned right back.

He was nearly in tears.

"Oh, wow!" he kept saying.

"It's too big," muttered Gurder, trying not to look. Like most of the nomes who had been born in the Store, he hated looking up and not seeing a ceiling. Angalo was the same, but more than being Outside he hated not going fast.

"I've seen them go up in the sky," said Masklin. "They really do fly. Honestly."

"Wow!"

It loomed over them, so big that you had to keep on stepping back and back to see how big it was. Rain glistened on it. The airport lights made smears of green and white bloom on its flanks. It wasn't a *thing*, it was a bit of shaped sky.

"Of course, they look smaller when they're a long way off," Masklin muttered.

He stared up at the plane. He'd never felt smaller in his life.

"I *want* one," moaned Angalo, clenching his fists. "*Look* at it. It looks as though it's going too fast even when it's standing still!"

"How do we get on it, then?" said Gurder.

"Can't you just see their faces back home if we turned up with this?" said Angalo.

"Yes. I can. Horribly clearly," said Gurder. "But how do we get on it?"

"We could . . ." Angalo began. He hesitated. "Why did you have to ruin everything?" he snapped.

"There's the holes where the wheels stick through," said Masklin. "I think we could climb up there."

"*No,*" said the Thing, which was tucked under Masklin's arm. "*You would not be able to breathe. You must be properly inside. Where the planes go, the air is thin.*"

"I should hope so," said Gurder, stoutly. "That's why it's air."

"*You would not be able to breathe,*" said the Thing patiently.

"Yes, I would," said Gurder. "I've always been able to breathe."

"You get more air close to the ground," said Angalo. "I read that in a book. You gets lots of air low down, and not much when you go up."

"Why not?" said Gurder.

"Dunno. It's frightened of heights, I guess."

Masklin waded through the puddles on the concrete so that he could see down the far side of the aircraft. Some way away a couple of humans were using some sort of machines to load boxes into a hole in the side of the plane. He walked back, around the huge tires, and squinted up at a long, high tube that stretched from the building.

He pointed.

"I think that's how humans are loaded onto it," he said.

"What, through a pipe? Like water?" said Angalo.

"It's better than standing out here getting wet, anyway," said Gurder. "I'm soaked through already."

"There are stairs and wires and things," said Masklin. "It shouldn't be too difficult to climb up there. There's bound to be a gap we can slip in by." He sniffed. "There always is," he added, "when humans build things."

"Let's do it!" said Angalo. "Oh, wow!"

"But you're not to try to steal it," said Masklin, as they helped the slightly plump Gurder lumber into a run. "It's going where we want to go anyway—"

"Not where I want to go," moaned Gurder. "I want to go home!"

"And you're not to try to drive it. There's not enough of us. Anyway, I expect it's a lot more complicated than a truck. It's a—do you know what it's called, Thing?"

"*A Concorde.*"

"There," said Masklin. "It's a Concorde. Whatever that is. And you've got to promise not to steal it."

Two

Concorde: It goes faster than a bullet and you get smoked salmon.

—From *A Scientific Encyclopedia for the Enquiring Young Nome* by Angalo de Haberdasheri.

Squeezing through a gap in the humans-walking-onto-planes pipe wasn't as hard as coming to terms with what was on the other side.

The floor of the sheds in the quarry had been bare boards or stamped earth. In the airport building it was squares of a sort of shiny stone. But here . . . Gurder flung himself face down and buried his nose in it.

"Carpet!" he said, almost in tears. "Carpet! I never thought I'd see you again!"

"Oh, get up," said Angalo, embarrassed at the Abbot acting like that in front of someone who, however much of a friend he was, hadn't been born a Store nome.

Gurder stood up awkwardly. "Sorry," he mumbled, brushing himself off. "Don't know what possessed me there. It just took me back, that's all. Real carpet. Haven't seen real carpet for *months.*"

He blew his nose noisily. "We had some beautiful carpets in the Store, you know. Beautiful. Some of them had patterns on them."

Masklin looked up the pipe. It was like one of the Store's corridors, and was quite brightly lit.

"Let's move on," he said. "It's too exposed here. Where are all the humans, Thing?"

"They will be arriving shortly."

"How does it *know*?" Gurder complained.

"It listens to other machines," said Masklin.

"There are also many computers on this plane," said the Thing.

"Well, that's nice," said Masklin vaguely. "You'll have someone to talk to, then."

"They are quite stupid," said the Thing, and managed to express disdain without actually having anything to express it with.

A few feet away the corridor opened into a new space. Masklin could see a curtain, and what looked like the edge of a chair.

"All right, Angalo," he said. "Lead the way. I know you want to."

It was two minutes later.

The three of them were sitting under a seat.

Masklin had never really thought about the insides of aircraft. He'd spent days up on the cliff behind the quarry, watching them take off. Of course, he'd assumed there were humans inside. Humans got everywhere. But he'd never really thought about the insides. If ever there was anything that looked made up of outsides, it was a plane.

But it had been too much for Gurder. He was in tears.

"Electric light," he moaned. "And more carpets! And big soft seats! They've even got antimacassars on them! And there isn't any mud *anywhere*! There are even *signs*!"

"There, there," said Angalo helplessly, patting him on the shoulder. "It was a *good* Store, I know." He looked up at Masklin.

"You've got to admit it's unsettling," he said. "I was expecting . . . well, wires and pipes and exciting levers and things. Not something like the Arnold Bros. Furnishings Department!"

"We shouldn't stay here," said Masklin. "There'll be humans all over the place pretty soon. Remember what the Thing said."

They helped Gurder up and trotted under the rows of seats with him between them. But it wasn't like the Store in one important way, Masklin realized. There weren't many places to hide. In the Store there was always something to get behind or under or wriggle through.

He could already hear distant sounds. In the

end they found a gap behind a curtain, in a part of the aircraft where there were no seats. Masklin crawled inside, pushing the Thing in front of him.

They weren't distant sounds now. They were very close. He turned his head, and saw a human foot a few inches away.

At the back of the gap there was a hole in the metal wall where some thick wires passed through. It was just big enough for Angalo and Masklin, and big enough for a terrified Gurder with the two of them pulling on his arms. There wasn't too much room, but at least they couldn't be seen.

They couldn't see, either. They lay packed together in the gloom, trying to make themselves comfortable on the wires.

After a while Gurder said, "I feel a bit better now."

Masklin nodded.

There were noises all around them. From somewhere far below came a series of metallic *clonks*. There was the mournful sound of human voices, and then a jolt.

"Thing?" he whispered.

"*Yes?*"

"What's happening?"

"*The plane is getting ready to become airborne.*"

"Oh."

"*Do you know what that means?*"

"No. Not really."

"It is going to fly in the air. 'Borne' means to be carried, and 'air' means air. To be borne in the air. Airborne."

Masklin could hear Angalo's breathing.

He settled himself as best he could between the metal wall and a thick bundle of wires, and stared into the darkness.

The nomes didn't speak. After a while there was a faint jerk and a sensation of movement.

Nothing else happened. It went on not happening.

Eventually Gurder, his voice trembling with terror, said, "Is it too late to get off, if we—?"

A sudden distant thundering noise finished the sentence for him. A dull rumbling shook everything around them very gently but very firmly.

Then there was a heavy pause, like the moment a ball must feel between the time it's thrown up and the time it starts to come down, and something picked up all three of them and slid them into a struggling heap. The floor tried to become the wall.

The nomes hung on to one another, stared into one another's faces, and screamed.

After a while, they stopped. There didn't seem much point in continuing. Besides, they were out of breath.

The floor very gradually became a proper floor again, and didn't show any further ambitions to become a wall.

Masklin pushed Angalo's foot off his neck.

"I think we're flying," he said.

"Is that what it was?" said Angalo weakly. "It looks kind of more graceful when you see it from the ground."

"Is anyone hurt?"

Gurder pulled himself upright.

"I'm all bruises," he said. He brushed himself down. And then, because there is no changing nomish nature, he added, "Is there any food around?"

They hadn't thought about food.

Masklin stared behind him into the tunnel of wires.

"Maybe we won't need any," he said, uncertainly. "How long will it take to get to Florida, Thing?"

"*The captain has just said it will be many hours,*" said the Thing.*

"We'll starve to death!" said Gurder.

"Maybe there's something to hunt?" said Angalo hopefully.

"I shouldn't think so," Masklin said. "This doesn't look a mouse kind of place."

"The humans'll have food," said Gurder. "Humans always have food."

"I *knew* you were going to say that," said Angalo.

---

* An hour lasts nearly as long as half a day, to a nome.

"It's just common sense."

"I wonder if we can see out a window?" said Angalo. "I'd like to see how fast we're going. All the trees and things whizzing past, and so on?"

"Look," said Masklin, before things got out of hand. "Let's just wait for a while, eh? Everyone calm down. Have a bit of a rest. *Then* maybe we can look for some food."

They settled down again. At least it was warm and dry. Back in the days when he'd lived in a hole in a bank Masklin had spent far too much time cold and wet to turn up his nose at a chance to sleep warm and dry.

He dozed.

Airborne.

Air . . . born . . .

Perhaps there were hundreds of nomes who lived in the airplanes in the same way that nomes had lived in the Store. Perhaps they got on with their lives under the carpeted floor somewhere, while they were whisked to all the places Masklin had seen on the only map the nomes had ever found. It had been in a pocket diary, and the names of the faraway places written on it were like magic—Africa, Australia, China, Equator, Printed in Hong Kong, Iceland. . . .

Perhaps they'd never looked out the windows. Perhaps they'd never known that they were moving at all.

He wondered if this was what Grimma had meant by all the stuff about the frogs in the flower. She'd read it in a book. You could live your whole life in some tiny place and think it was the whole world. The trouble was, he'd been angry. He hadn't wanted to listen.

Well, he was out of the flower now and no mistake.

The frog had brought some other young frogs to its spot among the leaves at the edge of the world of the flower.

They stared at the branch. There wasn't just one flower out there, there were dozens, although the frogs weren't able to think like this because frogs can't count beyond one.

They saw lots of ones.

They stared at them. Staring is one of the few things frogs are good at.

Thinking isn't. It would be nice to say that the tiny frogs thought long and hard about the new flower, about life in the old flower, about the need to explore, about the possibility that the world was bigger than a pool with petals around the edge.

In fact, what they thought was . . . *mipmip* . . . *mipmip* . . . *mipmip*.

But what they *felt* was too big for one flower to contain.

Carefully, slowly, not at all certain why, they plopped down onto the branch.

There was a polite beeping from the Thing.

"You may be interested to know," it said, *"that we've broken the sound barrier."*

Masklin turned wearily to the others.

"All right, own up," he said. "Who broke it?"

"Don't look at me," said Angalo. "I didn't touch anything."

Masklin crawled to the edge of the hole and peered out.

There were human feet out there. Female human feet, by the look of it. They usually were the ones with the less practical shoes.

You could learn a lot about humans by looking at their shoes. It was about all a nome had to look at, most of the time. The rest of the human was normally little more than the wrong end of a pair of nostrils, a long way up.

Masklin sniffed.

"There's food somewhere," he said.

"What kind?" said Angalo.

"Never mind what kind," said Gurder, pushing him out of the way. "Whatever it is, I'm going to *eat* it."

"Get back!" Masklin snapped, pushing the Thing into Angalo's arms. "I'll go! Angalo, don't let him go!"

He darted out, ran for the curtain, and slid behind it. After a few seconds, he moved just enough to let one eye and a frowning eyebrow show.

The room was some sort of food place. Human females were taking trays of food out of the wall. Nomish sense of smell is sharper than a fox's; it was all Masklin could do not to dribble. He had to admit it—it was all very well hunting and growing things, but what you got wasn't a patch on the food you found around humans.

One of the females put the last tray on a trolley and wheeled it past Masklin. The wheels were almost as tall as he was.

As it squeaked past, he jumped out of his hiding place and leapt onto it, squeezing himself among the bottles. It was a stupid thing to do, he knew. It was just better than being stuck in a hole with a couple of idiots.

Rows and rows of shoes. Some black, some brown. Some with laces, some without. Quite a few of them without feet in them, because the humans had taken them off.

Masklin looked up as the trolley inched forward.

Rows and rows of legs. Some in skirts, but most in trousers.

Masklin looked up farther. Nomes rarely saw humans sitting down.

Rows and rows of bodies, topped with rows and rows of heads with faces at the front. Rows and rows of—

Masklin crouched back among the bottles.

Grandson Richard, 39, was watching him.

It was the face in the newspaper. It had to be. There was the little beard, and the smiling mouth with lots of teeth in it. And the hair that looked as though it had been dramatically carved out of something shiny rather than grown in the normal way.

Grandson Richard. 39.

The face stared at him for a moment, and then looked away.

He can't have seen me, Masklin told himself. I'm hidden away here.

What will Gurder say when I tell him?

He'll go mad, that's what.

I think I'll keep it to myself for a while. That might be an amazingly good idea. We've got enough to worry about as it is.

Thirty-nine. Either there've been thirty-eight other Grandson Richards, and I don't think that's what it means, or it's a newspaper human way of saying he's thirty-nine years old. Nearly half as old as the Store. And the Store nomes say the Store is as old as the world. I know that can't be true, but . . .

I wonder what it feels like to live nearly *forever*?

He burrowed farther into the things on the shelf. Mostly they were bottles, but there were a few bags containing knobbly things a bit smaller than Masklin's fist. He stabbed at the paper with his knife until he'd cut a hole big enough, and pulled one of them out.

It was a salted peanut. Well, it was a start.

He grabbed the packet just as a hand reached past.

It was close enough to touch.

It was close enough to touch *him*.

He could see the red of its fingernails as they slid by him, closed slowly over another packet of nuts, and withdrew.

It dawned on Masklin later that the giving-out-food female wouldn't have been able to see him. She just reached down into the tray for what she knew would be there, and this almost certainly didn't include Masklin.

That's what he decided later. At the time, with a human hand almost brushing his head, it all looked a lot different. He took a running dive off the trolley, rolled when he hit the carpet, and scurried under the nearest seat.

He didn't even wait to catch his breath. Experience had taught him that it was when you stopped to catch your breath that things caught you. He charged from seat to seat, dodging giant feet, discarded shoes, dropped newspapers and bags. By the time he crossed the bit of aisle to the food-place, he was a blur even by nome standards. He didn't stop even when he reached the hole. He just leapt, and went through it without touching the sides.

"A peanut?" said Angalo. "Between three? That's not a mouthful each!"

"What do you suggest?" said Masklin, bitterly. "Do you want to go to the giving-out-food female and say, there's three small hungry people down here?"

Angalo stared at him. Masklin had got his breath back now, but was still very red in the face.

"You know, that could be worth a try," he said.

"What?"

"Well, if you were a human, would you expect to see nomes on a plane?" said Angalo.

"Of course I wouldn't."

"I bet you'd be amazed if you *did* see one, eh?"

"Are you suggesting we deliberately show ourselves to a human?" Gurder said suspiciously. "We've never done that, you know."

"I nearly did just now," said Masklin. "I won't do that again in a hurry!"

"We've always preferred to starve to death on one peanut, you mean?"

Gurder looked longingly at the piece of nut in his hand. They'd eaten peanuts in the Store, of course. Around Christmas Fayre, when the Food Hall was crammed with food you didn't normally see in the other seasons; they made a nice end to a meal. Probably they made a nice start to a meal too. What they didn't make was a meal.

"What's the plan?" he said, wearily.

One of the giving-out-food humans was pulling trays off a shelf when a movement made it look up. Its head turned very slowly.

Something small and black was being lowered down right by its ear.

It stuck tiny thumbs in small ears, wagged its fingers, and stuck out its tongue.

"*Thrrrrrrrp,*" said Gurder.

The tray in the human's hands crashed onto the floor in front of it. It made a long, drawn-out noise that sounded like a high-pitched foghorn, and backed away, raising its hands to its mouth. Finally it turned, very slowly, like a tree about to fall, and fled between the curtains.

When it came back, with another human being, the little figure had gone.

So had most of the food.

"I don't know when I last had smoked salmon," said Gurder happily.

"Mmmph," said Angalo.

"You're not supposed to eat it like that," said Gurder severely. "You're not supposed to shove it all in your mouth and then cut off whatever won't fit. Whatever will people think?"

" 'Sno people here," said Angalo indistinctly. " 'Sjust you an' Masklin."

Masklin cut the lid off a container of milk. It was practically nome-sized.

"This is more like it, eh?" said Gurder. "Proper food the natural way, out of tins and things. None of this having to clean the dirt off it, like in the quarry. And it's nice and warm in here too. It's the only way to travel. Anyone want some of this" —he prodded a dish vaguely, not sure of what was in it—"stuff?"

The others shook their heads. The dish contained something shiny and wobbly and pink with a cherry on it, and in some strange way it managed to look like something you wouldn't eat even if it was pushed onto your plate after a week's starvation diet.

"What does it taste like?" said Masklin, after Gurder had chewed a mouthful.

"Tastes like pink," said Gurder.*

"Anyone fancy the peanut to finish with?" said Angalo. He grinned. "No? I'll chuck it away, shall I?"

"No!" said Masklin. They looked at him. "Sorry," he said. "I mean, you shouldn't. It's wrong to waste good food."

---

* Little dishes of strange wobbly stuff tasting like pink turn up in nearly every meal on all airplanes. No one knows why. There's probably some sort of special religious reason.

"It's *wicked,*" said Gurder primly.

"Mmm. Don't know about wicked," said Masklin. "Never been very clear on wicked. But it's *stupid.* Put it in your pack. You never know when you might need it."

Angalo stretched his arms and yawned.

"A wash would be nice," he said.

"Didn't see any water," Masklin said. "There's probably a sink or a bathroom somewhere, but I wouldn't know where to start looking."

"Talking of bathrooms . . ." said Angalo.

"Right down the other end of the pipe, please," said Gurder.

"And keep away from any wiring," volunteered the Thing. Angalo nodded in a puzzled fashion, and crawled away into the darkness.

Gurder yawned and stretched his arms.

"Won't the giving-out-food humans look for us?" he said.

"I don't think so," said Masklin. "Back when we used to live Outside I'm sure humans saw us sometimes. I don't think they really believe their eyes. They wouldn't make those weird garden ornaments if they'd ever seen a *real* nome."

Gurder reached into his robe and pulled out the picture of Grandson Richard, 39. Even in the dim light in the pipe, Masklin recognized it as the human in the seat. He hadn't got creases on his face from being folded up, and he wasn't made up of hundreds of tiny dots, but apart from that. . . .

"Do you think he's here somewhere?" said Gurder wistfully.

"Could be. Could be," said Masklin, feeling wretched. "But, look, Gurder . . . maybe Angalo goes a bit too far, but he could be right. Maybe Grandson Richard, 39, is just another human being, you know. Probably humans did build the Store just for humans. Your ancestors just moved in because, well, it was warm and dry. And—"

"I'm not listening, you know," said Gurder. "I'm not going to be told that we're just things like rats and mice. We're special."

"The Thing is quite definite about us coming from somewhere else, Gurder," said Masklin meekly.

The Abbot folded up the picture. "Maybe we did. Maybe we didn't," he said. "That doesn't matter."

"Angalo thinks it matters if it's true."

"Don't see why. There's more than one kind of truth." Gurder shrugged. "I might say, you're just a lot of dust and juices and bones and hair, and that's true. And I might say, you're something inside your head that goes away when you die. That's true too. Ask the Thing."

Colored lights flickered across the Thing's surface.

Masklin looked shocked.

"I've *never* asked it that sort of question," he said.

"Why not? It's the first question *I'd* ask."

"It'll probably say something like 'Does not compute' or 'Inoperative parameters.' That's what it says when it doesn't know and doesn't want to admit it. Thing?"

The Thing didn't reply. Its lights changed their pattern.

"Thing?" Masklin repeated.

"I am monitoring communications."

"It often does that when it's feeling bored," said Masklin to Gurder. "It just sits there listening to invisible messages in the air. Pay attention, Thing. This is important. We want—"

The lights moved. A lot of them went red.

"Thing! We—"

The Thing made the little clicking noise that was the equivalent of clearing its throat.

"A nome has been seen in the pilot's cabin."

"Listen, Thing, we— What?"

"I repeat: A nome has been seen in the pilot's cabin."

Masklin looked around wildly.

"Angalo?"

"That is an extreme probability," said the Thing.

Three

Traveling Humans: Large, nomelike creatures. Many humans spend a lot of time traveling from place to place, which is odd because there are usually too many humans at the place they're going to anyway. Also see under *Animals, Intelligence, Evolution,* and *Custard.*

—From *A Scientific Encyclopedia for the Enquiring Young Nome* by Angalo de Haberdasheri.

The sound of Masklin's and Gurder's voices echoed up and down the pipe as they scrambled over the wires.

"I *thought* he was taking too long!"

"You shouldn't have let him go off by himself! You know what he's like about driving things!"

"*I* shouldn't have let him?"

"He's just got no sense of—which way now? We're been searching for *ages.*"

Angalo had said he thought the inside of a plane

would be a mass of wires and pipes. He was nearly right. The nomes squeezed their way through a narrow, cable-hung world under the floor.

"I'm too old for this! There comes a time in a nome's life when he shouldn't crawl around the inside of terrible flying machines!"

"How many time have you done it?"

"Once too often!"

"We are getting closer," said the Thing.

"This is what comes of showing ourselves! It's a Judgment," declared Gurder.

"Whose?" said Masklin grimly, helping him up.

"What do you mean?"

"There has to be someone to make a judgment!"

"I meant just a judgment in general!"

Masklin stopped.

"Where to now, Thing?"

"The message told the giving-out-food humans that a strange little creature was on the flight deck," said the Thing. *"That is where we are. There are many computers here."*

"They're talking to you, are they?"

"A little. They are like children. Mostly they listen," said the Thing smugly. *"They are not very intelligent."*

"What are we going to *do*?" said Gurder.

"We're going to . . ." Masklin hesitated. The word "rescue" was looming up somewhere in the sentence ahead.

It was a good, dramatic word.

He longed to say it. The trouble was that there was another, simpler, nastier word a little farther beyond.

It was "how"?

"I don't think they'd try to hurt him," he said, hoping it was true. "Maybe they'll put him somewhere. We ought to find somewhere where we can see what's happening." He looked helplessly at the wires and intricate bits of metal in front of them.

"You'd better let me lead, then," said Gurder, in a matter-of-fact voice.

"Why?"

"You might be very good at wide-open spaces," said the Abbot, pushing past him. "But in the Store we know all about getting around inside things."

He rubbed his hands together.

"Right," he said, and then grabbed a cable and slid through a gap Masklin hadn't even noticed was there.

"Used to do this sort of thing when I was a boy," he said. "We used to get up to all sorts of tricks."

"Yes?" said Masklin.

"Down this way, I think. Mind the wires. Oh, yes. Up and down the elevator shafts, in and out of the telephone switchboard—"

"I thought you always said kids spent far too much time running around and getting into mischief these days?"

"Ah. Yes. Well, *that's* juvenile delinquency," said Gurder sternly. "It's quite different from our youthful high spirits. Let's try up here."

They crawled between two warm metal walls. There was daylight ahead.

Masklin and Gurder lay down and pulled themselves forward.

There was an odd-shaped room, not a lot bigger than the cab of the Truck itself. Like the cab, it was really just a space where the human drivers fitted into the machinery.

There was a *lot* of that.

It covered the walls and ceiling. Lights and switches, dials and levers. Masklin thought, if Dorcas were here, we'd never get him to leave. Angalo's here somewhere, and we want *him* to leave.

There were two humans kneeling on the floor. One of the giving-out-food females was standing by them. There was a lot of mooing and growling going on.

"Human talking," muttered Masklin. "I wish we could understand it."

"Very well," said the Thing. *"Stand by."*

"You can understand human noises?"

"Certainly. They're only nome noises slowed down."

"What? *What?* You never told us that! You never told us that before!"

"There are many billions of things I have not told you. Where would you like me to start?"

"You can start by telling me what they're saying now," said Masklin. "Please?"

"One of the humans has just said, 'It must have been a mouse or something,' and the other one said, 'You show me a mouse wearing clothes, and I'll admit it was a mouse.' And the giving-out-food female said, 'It was no mouse I saw. It blew a raspberry at me (exclamation).'"

"What's a raspberry?"

"The small red fruit of the plant Rubus idaeus."

Masklin turned to Gurder.

"Did you?"

"Me? What fruit? Listen, if there'd been any fruit around I'd have eaten it. I just went *'thrrrrrr-rrp.'"*

"One of the humans has just said, 'I looked around and there it was, staring out the window.'"

"That's Angalo all right," said Gurder.

"Now the other kneeling-down human has said, 'Well, whatever it is, it's behind this panel and it can't go anywhere.'"

"It's taking off a bit of the wall!" said Masklin. "Oh, no! It's reaching inside!"

The human mooed.

"The human said, 'It bit me! The little devil bit me!'" said the Thing, conversationally.

"Yep. That's Angalo," said Gurder. "His father was like that too. A fighter in a tight corner."

"But they don't know what they've got!" said

Masklin urgently. "They've seen him, but he ran away! They're arguing about it! They don't really believe in nomes! If we can get him out before he's caught, they're bound to think it was a mouse or something!"

"I suppose we could get around there inside the walls," said Gurder. "But it'd take too long."

Masklin looked desperately around the cabin. Besides the three people trying to catch Angalo there were two humans up at the front. They must be the drivers, he thought.

"I'm right out of ideas," he said. "Can you think of anything, Thing?"

"There is practically no limit to what I can think of."

"I *mean*, is there anything you can do to help us rescue Angalo?"

"Yes."

"You'd better do it, then."

"Yes."

A moment later they heard the low clanging of alarms. Lights began to flash. The drivers shouted and leaned forward and started doing things to switches.

"What's going on?" said Masklin.

"It is possible that the humans are startled that they are no longer flying this machine," said the Thing.

"They're not? Who is, then?"

The lights rippled smoothly across the Thing.

"I am."

* * *

One of the frogs fell off the branch, and disappeared quietly into the leafy canopy far below. Since very small light animals can fall a long way without being hurt, it's quite likely that it survived in the forest world under the tree and had the second most interesting experience any tree frog has ever had.

The rest of them crawled onward. They were going to have the *most* interesting experience any frog ever had anywhere, one which would go down in frog history and be remembered for . . . maybe even for *minutes.*

Masklin helped Gurder along another metal channel full of wires. Overhead, they could hear human feet and the growling of humans in trouble.

"I don't think they're very happy about it," said Gurder.

"But they haven't got time to look for something that was probably a mouse," said Masklin.

"It's not a mouse, it's Angalo!"

"But afterward they'll *think* it was a mouse. I don't think humans want to know things that disturb them."

"Sound just like nomes to me," said Gurder.

Masklin looked at the Thing under his arm.

"Are you really driving the Concorde?" he said.

"Yes."

"I thought to drive things you had to turn

wheels and change gears and things?" said Masklin.

"That is all done by machines. The humans press buttons and turn wheels just to tell machines what to do."

"So what are *you* doing, then?"

"I," said the Thing, *"am being in charge."*

Masklin listened to the muted thunder of the engines.

"Is that hard?" he said.

"Not in itself. However, the humans keep trying to interfere."

"I think we'd better find Angalo quickly, then," said Gurder. "Come on."

They inched their way along another cable tunnel.

"They ought to thank us for letting our Thing do their job for them," said Gurder solemnly.

"I don't think they see it like that, exactly," said Masklin.

"We are flying at a height of 55,000 feet at 1,352 miles per hour," said the Thing.

When they didn't comment, it added, *"That's very high and very fast."*

"That's good," said Masklin, who realized that some sort of remark was expected.

"Very, very fast."

The two nomes squeezed through the gap between a couple of metal plates.

"Faster than a bullet, in fact."

"Amazing," said Masklin.

"*Twice the speed of sound in this atmosphere,*" the Thing went on.

"Wow."

"*I wonder if I can put it another way,*" said the Thing, and it managed to sound slightly annoyed. "*It could get from the Store to the quarry in under fifteen seconds.*"

"Good job we didn't meet it coming the other way, then," said Masklin.

"Oh, stop teasing it," said Gurder. "It wants you to tell it it's a good boy—Thing," he corrected himself.

"*I do not,*" said the Thing, rather more quickly than usual. "*I was merely pointing out that this is a very specialized machine and requires skillful control.*"

"Perhaps you shouldn't talk so much, then," said Masklin.

The Thing rippled its lights at him.

"That was nasty," said Gurder.

"Well, I've spent a year doing what the Thing's told me and I've never had so much as a 'thank you,'" said Masklin. "How high are 55,000 feet, anyway?"

"*Ten miles. Twice as far as the distance from the Store to the quarry.*"

Gurder stopped.

"Up?" he said. "We're that far *up*?"

He looked down at the floor.

"Oh," he said.

"Now, don't *you* start," said Masklin quickly.

"We've got enough problems with Angalo. Stop holding on to the wall like that!"

Gurder had gone white.

"We must be as high as all those fluffy white cloud things," he breathed.

"No," said the Thing.

"That's some comfort, then," said Gurder.

"They're all a long way below us."

"Oh."

Masklin grabbed the Abbot's arm.

"Angalo, remember?" he said.

Gurder nodded slowly and inched his way forward, holding on to things with his eyes closed.

"We mustn't lose our heads," said Masklin. "Even if we *are* up so high." He looked down. The metal below him was quite solid. You needed to use imagination to see through it to the ground below.

The trouble was that he had a very good imagination.

"Ugh," he said. "Come on, Gurder. Give me your hand."

"It's right in front of you."

"Sorry. Didn't see it with my eyes shut."

They spent what seemed like ages cautiously moving up and down among the wiring, until eventually Gurder said, "It's no good. There isn't a hole big enough to get through. He'd have found it if there was."

"Then we've got to find a way into the cab and get him out that way," said Masklin.

"With all those humans in there?"

"They'll be too busy to notice us. Right, Thing?"

"Right."

There is a place so far up there is no down.

A little lower, a white dart seared across the top of the sky, outrunning the night, overtaking the sun, crossing in a few hours an ocean that was once the edge of the world.

Masklin lowered himself carefully to the floor and crept forward. The humans weren't even looking in his direction.

I hope the Thing really knows how to drive this plane, he thought.

He sidled along toward the panels where, with any luck, Angalo was hiding.

This wasn't right. He hated being exposed like this. Of course, it had probably been worse in the days when he used to have to hunt alone. If anything had caught him then, he would never have known it. He'd have been a mouthful. Whereas no one knew what humans would do to a nome if they caught one.

He darted into the blessed shadows.

"Angalo!" he whispered.

After a while a voice from behind the wiring said, "Who is it?"

Masklin straightened up.

"How many guesses do you want?" he said in his normal voice.

Angalo dropped down.

"They chased me!" he said. "And one of them stuck its arm—"

"I know. Come on, while they're busy."

"What's happening?" said Angalo as they hurried out into the light.

"The Thing is flying us."

"How? It's got no arms. It can't change gears or anything—"

"Apparently it's being bossy to the computers that do all that. Come *on.*"

"I looked out the window," bubbled Angalo. "There's sky all over the place!"

"Don't remind me," said Masklin.

"Let me just have one more look—" Angalo began.

"Listen, Gurder's waiting for us and we don't want any more trouble—"

"But this is better than any truck—"

There was a strangled kind of noise.

The nomes looked up.

One of the humans was watching them. Its mouth was open and it had an expression on its face of someone who is going to have a lot of difficulty explaining what they have just seen, especially to themselves.

The human was already getting to its feet.

Angalo and Masklin looked at one another.

"Run!" they shouted.

Gurder was lurking suspiciously in a patch of shadow by the door when they came past, arms and legs going like pistons. He caught up the skirts of his robe and scurried after them.

"What's happening! What's happening?"

"There's a human after us!"

"Don't leave me behind! Don't leave me behind!"

Masklin was just ahead of the other two as they raced up the aisle between the rows of humans, who paid no attention at all to three tiny blurs running between the seats.

"We shouldn't have . . . stood around . . . looking!" Masklin gasped.

"We might . . . never . . . have a chance . . . like that again!" panted Angalo.

"You're *right*!"

The floor tilted slightly.

"*Thing!* What are you doing!"

"*Creating a distraction.*"

"Don't! Everyone this way!"

Masklin darted between two seats, around a pair of giant shoes, and threw himself flat on the carpet. The others hurled themselves down behind him.

Two huge human feet were a few inches away from them.

Masklin pulled the Thing up close to his face.

"Let them have their airplane back!" he said.

"I was hoping to be allowed to land it," said the Thing. Even though its voice was always flat and expressionless, Masklin still thought that it sounded wistful.

"Do you know how to land one of these things?" said Masklin.

"I should like the opportunity to learn—"

"Let them have it back right *now!*"

There was a faint lurch and a change in the pattern of the lights on the Thing's surface. Masklin breathed out.

"Now, will everyone act sensibly for five minutes?" he said.

"Sorry, Masklin," said Angalo. He tried to look apologetic, but it didn't work. Masklin recognized the wide-eyed, slightly mad smile of someone very nearly in their own personal heaven. "It was just that . . . do you know it's even blue below us? It's like there's no ground down there at all! And—"

"If the Thing tries any more flying lessons we might all find out if that's true," said Masklin gloomily. "So let's just sit down and be quiet, shall we?"

They sat in silence for a long time, under the seat.

Then Gurder said, "That human there has got a hole in its sock."

"What about it?" said Angalo.

"Dunno, really. It's just that you never think of humans as having holes in their socks."

"Where you get socks, holes aren't far behind," said Masklin.

"They're good socks, though," said Angalo.

Masklin stared at them. They just looked like basic socks to him. Nomes in the store used them as sleeping bags.

"How can you tell?" he said.

"They're Hi-style Odorprufe," said Angalo. "Guaranteed 85% Polysomething. We used to sell them in the Store. They cost a lot more than other socks. Look, you can see the label."

Gurder sighed.

"It was a good Store," he muttered.

"And those shoes," said Angalo, pointing to the great white shapes like beached boats a little way away. "See them? Crucial Street Drifters with Real Rubber Soul. Very expensive."

"Never approved of them, myself," said Gurder. "Too flashy. I preferred Mens, Brown, Laced. A nome can get a good night's sleep in one of those."

"Those Drifter things are Store shoes, too, are they?" said Masklin, carefully.

"Oh, yes. Special range."

"Hmm."

Masklin got up and walked over to a large leather bag half wedged under the seat. The others watched him scramble up it and then pull himself up until he could, very quickly, glance over the armrest. He slid back down.

"Well, well," he said, in a mad, cheerful voice.

"That's a Store bag, isn't it?" he said.

Gurder and Angalo gave it a critical look.

"Never spent much time in Travel Accessories," said Angalo, "but now that you mention it, it could be the Special Calfskin Carry-on Bag."

"For the Discerning Executive?" Gurder added. "Yes. Could be."

"Have you wondered how we're going to get off?" said Masklin.

"Same way as we got on?" said Angalo, who hadn't.

"I think that could be difficult. I think the humans might have other ideas," said Masklin. "I think, in fact, they might start looking for us. Even if they think we're mice. I wouldn't put up with mice on something like this if I were them. You know what mice are like for widdling on wires. Could be dangerous when you're ten miles high, a mouse going to the bathroom inside your computer. So I think the humans will take it very seriously. So we ought to get off when the humans do."

"We'd get stamped on!" said Angalo.

"I was thinking maybe we could sort of . . . get in this bag, sort of thing," said Masklin.

"Ridiculous!" said Gurder.

Masklin took a deep breath.

"It belongs to Grandson Richard, 39, you see," he said.

"I checked," he added, watching the expressions on their faces. "I saw him before, and he's in the seat up there. Grandson Richard," he went on, "39. He's up there right now. Reading a paper. Up there. Him."

Gurder had gone red. He prodded Masklin with a finger. "Do you expect me to believe," he said, "that Richard Arnold, the grandson of Arnold Bros. (est. 1905), has *holes* in his *socks*?"

"That'd make them holy socks," said Angalo. "Sorry. Sorry. Just trying to lighten the mood a bit. You don't have to glare at me like that."

"Climb up and see for yourself," said Masklin. "I'll help you. Only be careful."

They hoisted Gurder up.

He came down quietly.

"Well?" said Angalo.

"It's got *R. A.* in gold letters on the bag too," said Masklin. He made frantic signs to Angalo. Gurder was looking as though he had seen a ghost.

"Yes, you can get that," said Angalo, hurriedly. " 'Gold Monogram at Only Five Ninety-nine Extra,' it used to say on the sign."

"*Speak* to us, Gurder," said Masklin. "Don't just sit there looking like that."

"This is a very solemn moment for me," said Gurder.

"I thought I could cut through some of the stitching and we could get in at the bottom," said Masklin.

"I am not worthy," said Gurder.

"Probably not," said Angalo cheerfully. "But we won't tell anyone."

"And Grandson Richard, 39, will be helping us, you see," said Masklin, hoping that Gurder was in a state to take all this in. "He won't know it, but he'll be helping us. So it'll all be right. Probably it's *meant.*"

Not meant *by* anyone, he told himself conscientiously. Just meant in general.

Gurder considered this.

"Well, all right," he said. "But no cutting the bag. We can get in through the zipper, all right?"

They did. It stuck a bit halfway, since zippers always do, but it didn't take long to get an opening big enough for the nomes to climb down inside.

"What shall we do if he looks in?" said Angalo.

"Nothing," said Masklin. "Just smile, I suppose."

The tree frogs were far out on the branch now. What had looked like a smooth expanse of gray-green wood was, close up, a maze of rough bark, roots, and clumps of moss. It was unbearably frightening for frogs who had spent their lives in a world with petals around it.

But they crawled onward. They didn't know the meaning of the word "retreat." If it came to that, they didn't know the meaning of the word "bromeliad." Or "frog." Or any other word.

Four

Hotels: A place where *traveling humans* are parked at night. Other humans bring them food, including the famous *bacon, lettuce, and tomato sandwich.* There are beds and towels and special things that rain on humans to get them clean.

    —From *A Scientific Encyclopedia for the Enquiring Young Nome* by Angalo de Haberdasheri.

Blackness.

"It's very dark in here, Masklin."

"Yes, and I can't get comfortable."

"Well, you'll have to make the best of it."

"A hairbrush! I've just sat down on a hairbrush!"

"We will be landing shortly."

"Good."

"And there's a tube of something—"

"I'm hungry. Isn't there anything to eat?"

"I've still got that peanut."

"Where? Where?"

"Now you've made me drop it."

"Gurder?"

"Yes?"

"*What* are you *doing*? Are you cutting something?"

"He's cutting a hole in his sock."

Silence.

"Well? What of it? I can if I want to. It's my sock."

More silence.

"I shall just feel better for doing it."

Still more silence.

"It's just a human, Gurder. There's nothing special about it."

"We're in its bag, aren't we?"

"Yes, but you said yourself that Arnold Bros. is something in our heads. Didn't you?"

"Yes."

"Well, then?"

"This just makes me feel better, that's all. Subject closed."

"*We're about to land.*"

"How will we know when—"

"*I am sure I could have done it better. Eventually.*"

"Is this the Florida place? Angalo, get your foot out of my face."

"*Yes. This country traditionally welcomes immigrants.*"

"Is that what we are?"

"Technically you are en route to another destination."

"Which?"

"The stars."

"Oh. Thing?"

"Yes?"

"Is there any record of nomes being here before?"

"What do you mean? *We're* the nomes!"

"Yes, but there may have been others."

"We're all that there is! Aren't we?"

Tiny colored lights flickered in the darkness of the bag.

"Thing?" Masklin repeated.

"I am searching available data. Conclusion: no reliable sighting of nomes. All recorded immigrants have been in excess of four inches high."

"Oh. I just wondered. I wondered if we were all that there was."

"You heard the Thing. No reliable sightings, it said."

"No one saw *us* until today."

"Thing, do you know what happens next?"

"We will pass through Immigration and Customs. Are you now, or have you ever been, a member of a subversive organization?"

Silence.

"What, us? Why are you asking us that?"

"It is the sort of question that gets asked. I am monitoring communications."

"Oh. Well. I don't think we have. Have we?"

"No."

"No."

"No. I didn't think we were. What does 'subversive' mean?"

"The question seeks to establish whether you've come here to overthrow the Government of the United States."

"I don't think we want to do that. Do we?"

"No."

"No."

"No, we don't. They don't have to worry about us."

"Very clever idea, though."

"What is?"

"Asking the questions when people arrive. If anyone was coming here to do some subversive overthrowing, everyone'd be down on him like a pound of bricks as soon as he answered 'Yes.'"

"It's a sneaky trick, isn't it?" said Angalo, in an admiring tone of voice.

"No, we don't want to do any overthrowing," said Masklin to the Thing. "We just want to steal one of their going-straight-up jets. What are they called again?"

"Space shuttles."

"Right. And then we'll be off. We don't want to cause any trouble."

The bag bumped around and was put down.

There was a tiny sawing noise, totally unheard

amid the noise of the airport. A very small hole appeared in the leather. An eye appeared.

"What's he doing?" said Gurder.

"Stop pushing," said Masklin. "I can't concentrate. Now it looks like we're in a line of humans."

"We've been waiting for *ages,* " said Angalo.

"I expect everyone's being asked if they're going to do any overthrowing," said Gurder wisely.

"I hardly like to bring this up," said Angalo, "but how are we going to find this shuttle?"

"We'll sort that out when the time comes," said Masklin uncertainly.

"The time's come," said Angalo. "Hasn't it?"

Masklin shrugged helplessly.

"You didn't think we'd arrive in this Florida place and there'd be signs up saying 'This way to Space,' did you?" said Angalo sarcastically.

Masklin hoped his thoughts didn't show up on his face. "Of course not," he said.

"Well, what do we do next?" Angalo insisted.

"We . . . we . . . we ask the Thing," said Masklin. He looked relieved. "That's what we'll do. Thing?"

"*Yes?*"

Masklin shrugged. "What do we do next?"

"Now that," said Angalo, "is what I call planning."

The bag shifted. Grandson Richard, 39, was moving up the line.

"Thing? I said, what do we do—"

"Nothing."

"How can we do nothing?"

"By performing an absence of activity."

"What good is that?"

"The paper said Richard Arnold was going to Florida for the launch of the communications satellite. Therefore, he is going to the place where the satellite is now. Ergo, we will go with him."

"Who's Ergo?" said Gurder, looking around.

The Thing flickered its lights at him.

"It means 'therefore,'" it said.

Masklin looked doubtful. "Do you think he'll take this bag with him?"

"Uncertain."

There wasn't a lot in the bag, Masklin had to admit. It contained mainly socks, papers, a few odds and ends like hairbrushes, and a book called *The Spy with No Trousers*. This last item had caused them some concern when the bag had been unzipped just after the plane landed, but Grandson Richard, 39, had thrust it in among the papers without glancing inside. Now that there was a little light to see by, Angalo was trying to read it. Occasionally he'd mutter under his breath.

"It seems to me," Masklin said eventually, "that Grandson Richard, 39, isn't going to go straight off to watch the satellite fly away. I'm sure he'll go somewhere and sleep first. Do you know when this shuttle jet flies, Thing?"

"Uncertain. I can talk to other computers only when

they are within my range. The computers here know only about airport matters."

"He's going to have to go to sleep soon, anyway," said Masklin. "Humans sleep through most of the night. I think that's when we'd better leave the bag."

"And then we can talk to him," said Gurder.

The others stared at him.

"Well, that's why we came, isn't it?" said the Abbot. "Originally? To ask him to save the quarry?"

"He's a *human*!" snapped Angalo. "Even you must realize that by now! He's not going to help us! Why should he help us? He's just a human whose ancestors built a store! Why do you go on believing he's some sort of great big nome in the sky?"

"Because I haven't got anything else to believe in!" shouted Gurder. "And if you don't believe in Grandson Richard, 39, why are you in his bag?"

"That's just a coincidence—"

"You *always* say that! You always say it's just a coincidence!"

The bag moved, so they lost their balance again and fell over.

"We're moving," said Masklin, still peering out the hole and almost glad of anything that would stop the argument. "We're walking across the floor. There's a lot of humans out there. A *lot* of humans."

"There always are," sighed Gurder.

"Some of them are holding up signs with names on them."

"That's just like humans," Gurder added.

The nomes were used to humans with signs. Some of the humans in the Store used to wear their names all the time. Humans had strange long names, like Mrs. J. E. Williams Supervisor and Hello My Name Is Tracey. No one knew why humans had to wear their names. Perhaps they'd forget them otherwise.

"Hang on," said Masklin. "This can't be right. One of them is holding up a sign saying RICHARD ARNOLD. We're walking toward it! We're talking to it!"

The deep muffled rumble of the human voice rolled above the nomes like thunder.

Hoom-voom-boom?

Foom-boom-zoom-boom.

*Hoom-zoom-*boom-*foom?*

Boom!

"Can you understand it, Thing?" said Masklin.

"Yes. The one with the sign is here to take our human to a hotel. It's a place where humans sleep and are fed. All the rest of it is just the things humans say to each other to make sure that they're still alive."

"What do you mean?" said Masklin.

"They say things like 'How are you' and 'Have a nice day' and 'What do you think of this weather, then?' What these sounds mean is: I am alive and so are you."

"Yes, but nomes say the same sorts of things, Thing. It's called getting along with people. You might find it worth a try."

The bag swung sideways and hit something. The nomes clung desperately to the insides. Angalo clung with one hand. He was trying to keep his place in the book.

"I'm getting hungry again," said Gurder. "Isn't there anything to eat in this bag?"

"There's some toothpaste."

"I'll give the toothpaste a miss, thanks."

Now there was a rumbling noise. Angalo looked up. "I know *that* sound," he said. "Infernal combustion engine. We're in a vehicle."

"*Again?*" said Gurder.

"We'll get out as soon as we can," said Masklin.

"What kind of truck is it, Thing?" said Gurder.

"*It is a helicopter.*"

"It's certainly noisy," said Gurder, who had never come across the word.

"It is a plane without wings," said Angalo, who had.

Gurder gave this a few moments' careful and terrified thought.

"Thing?" he said, slowly.

"*Yes?*"

"What keeps it up in the—" Gurder began.

"*Science.*"

"Oh. Well. Science? Good. That's all right, then."

* * *

The noise went on for a long time. After a while it became part of the nomes' world, so that when it stopped the silence came as a shock.

They lay in the bottom of the bag, too discouraged even to talk. They felt the bag being carried, put down, picked up, carried again, put down, picked up one more time, and then thrown onto something soft.

And then there was blessed stillness.

Eventually Gurder's voice said: "All right. What *flavor* toothpaste?"

Masklin found the Thing among the heap of paper clips, dust, and screwed up bits of paper at the bottom of the bag.

"Any idea where we are, Thing?" he said.

"Room 103, Cocoa Beach New Horizons Hotel," said the Thing. *"I am monitoring communications."*

Gurder pushed past Masklin. "I've got to get out," he said. "I can't stand it in here anymore. Give me a leg up, Angalo. I reckon I can just reach the top of the bag."

There was the long, drawn-out rumble of the zipper. Light flooded in as the bag was opened. The nomes dived for whatever cover was available.

Masklin watched a hand taller than he was reached down, close around the smaller bag with the toothpaste and flannel in it, and pull it out.

The nomes didn't move.

After a while there came the distant sound of rushing water.

The nomes still didn't move.

Boom-boom foom zoom-boom-boom, choom zoom boooom . . .

The human noise rose above the gushing. It echoed even more than normal.

"It . . . sounds like it's . . . singing?" whispered Angalo.

Hoom . . . hoom-boom-boom boom . . . zoom-boom-boom HOOOooooOOOmmm. Boom.

"What's happening, Thing?" Masklin hissed.

"He has gone into a room to have water showering on himself," said the Thing.

"What does it want to do that for?"

"I assume he wants to keep clean."

"So is it safe to get out of the bag now?"

" 'Safe' is a relative word."

"What? What? Like 'uncle,' you mean?"

"I mean that nothing is totally safe. But I suggest that the human will be wetting himself for some time."

"Yeah. There's a lot of human to clean," said Angalo. "Come on. Let's do it."

The bag was lying on a bed. It was easy enough to climb down the covers onto the floor.

Hoom-hoom booOOOOM boom . . .

"What do we do now?" said Angalo.

"After we've eaten, that is," said Gurder firmly.

Masklin trotted across the thick carpet. There was a tall glass door in the nearest wall. It was slightly open, letting in a warm breeze and the sounds of the night.

A human would have heard the click and buzz of crickets and other small mysterious creatures whose role in life is to sit in bushes all night and make noises that are a lot bigger than they are. But nomes hear sounds slowed down and stretched out and deeper, like a record player on the wrong speed. The dark was full of the thud and growl of the wilderness.

Gurder joined Masklin and squinted anxiously into the blackness.

"Could you go out there and see if there is something to eat?" he said.

"I've a horrible feeling," said Masklin, "that if I go out there now there *will* be something to eat, and it'll be me."

Behind them the human voice sang on.

Boom-boom-boom—BOOOoooMMM womp . . .

"What's the human singing about, Thing?" said Masklin.

"It is a little difficult to follow. However, it appears that the singer wishes it to be known that he did something his way."

"Did what?"

"Insufficient data at this point. But whatever it was, he did it at a) each step on life's highway and b) not in a shy way."

There was a knock at the door. The singing

stopped. So did the gushing of the water. The nomes ran for the shadows.

"Sounds a bit dangerous," Angalo whispered. "Walking along highways, I mean. Each step along life's sidewalk would be safer."

Grandson Richard, 39, came out of the shower room with a towel around his waist. He opened the door. Another human, with all his clothes on, came in with a tray. There was a brief exchange of hoots, and the clothed human put down the tray and went out again. Grandson Richard, 39, disappeared into the shower room again.

Buh-buh buh-buh boom hoOOOOmm . . .

"Food!" Gurder whispered. "I can smell it! There's food on that tray!"

"*A bacon, lettuce, and tomato sandwich with cole-slaw,*" said the Thing. "*And coffee. And orange juice.*"

"How did you know?" said all three nomes in unison.

"*He ordered it when he checked in.*"

"Coleslaw!" moaned Gurder ecstatically. "Bacon! *Coffee!*"

"And orange juice," said Angalo. "Hah!"

Masklin stared upward. The tray had been left on the edge of a table.

There was a lamp near it. Masklin had lived in the Store long enough to know that where there was a lamp, there was a wire.

He'd never found a wire he couldn't climb.

Regular meals, that was the problem. He'd

never been used to them. When he'd lived Outside, he'd got accustomed to going for days without food and then, when food *did* turn up, eating until he was greasy to the eyebrows. But the Store nomes expected something to eat several times an hour. The Store nomes ate all the time. They only had to miss half a dozen meals and they started to complain.

"I think I could get up there," he said.

"Yes. Yes," said Gurder.

"But is it all right to eat Grandson Richard's sandwich?" Masklin added.

Gurder opened his eyes. He blinked.

"That's an important theological point," he muttered. "But I'm too hungry to think about it, so let's eat it first, and then if it turns out to be wrong to eat it, I promise to be very sorry."

Boom-boom whop whop, foom boom . . .

"The human says that the end is now near and he is facing a curtain," the Thing translated. *"This may be a shower curtain."*

Masklin pulled himself up the wire and onto the table, feeling very exposed.

It was obvious that the Floridians had a different idea about sandwiches. Sandwiches had been sold back in the Store's Food Hall. The word meant something thin between two slices of damp bread. Floridian sandwiches, on the other hand, filled up an entire tray and if there was any bread it was lurking deep in a jungle of cress and lettuce.

He looked down.

"Hurry up!" said Angalo. "The water's stopped again!"

Boom-boom boom whop boom whop . . .

Masklin pushed aside a drift of green stuff, grabbed the sandwich, hauled it to the edge of the tray and pushed it down onto the floor.

Foom boom boom HOOOOooooOOOOmmmmm-WHOP.

The shower room door opened.

"Come on! Come *on*!" Angalo yelled.

Grandson Richard, 39, came out. He took a few steps, and stopped.

He looked at Masklin.

Masklin looked at him.

There are times when Time itself pauses.

Masklin realized that he was standing at one of those points where History takes a deep breath and decides what to do next.

I can stay here, he thought. I can use the Thing to translate, and I can try to explain everything to him. I can tell him how important it is for us to have a home of our own. I can ask him if he can do something to help the nomes in the quarry. I can tell him how the Store nomes thought that his grandfather created the World. He'll probably enjoy knowing that. He looks friendly, for a human.

He *might* help us.

Or he'll trap us somehow, and call other humans, and they'll all start milling around and mooing, and we'll be put in a cage or something, and prodded. It'll be just like the Concorde drivers. They probably didn't want to hurt us, they just didn't understand what we were. And we haven't got time to let them find out.

It's their world, not ours.

It's too risky. No. I never realized it before, but we've got to do it *our* way.

Grandson Richard, 39, slowly reached out a hand and said, *Whoomp?*

Masklin took a running jump.

Nomes can fall quite a long way without being hurt, and in any case a bacon, lettuce, and tomato sandwich broke his fall.

There was a blur of activity and the sandwich rose on three pairs of legs. It raced across the floor, leaking mayonnaise.

Grandson Richard, 39, threw a towel at it. He missed.

The sandwich leapt over the doorway and vanished into the chirping, velvety, dangerous night.

There were other dangers besides falling off the branch. One of the frogs was eaten by a lizard. Several others turned back as soon as they were out of the shade of their bromeliad because, as they pointed out . . . *mipmip* . . . *mipmip*. . . .

The frog in the lead looked back at his dwindling group. There was one . . . and one . . . and one . . . and one . . . and one, which added

up to—it wrinkled its forehead in the effort of cal-
culation—yes, one.

Some of the one were getting frightened. The
leading frog realized that if they were ever going
to get to the new flower and survive there, there'd
need to be a lot more than one frog. They need at
least one, or possibly even one. He gave them a
croak of encouragement.

Mipmip, he said.

Five

Florida (or *Floridia*): A place where *alligators, long-necked turtles,* and *space shuttles* may be found. A place that is warm and wet, and there are geese. Only foolish people think it is really an orange drink. *Bacon, lettuce, and tomato sandwiches* may be found here also. A lot more interesting than many other places. The shape when seen from the air is like a bit stuck on a bigger bit.

—From *A Scientific Encyclopedia for the Enquiring Young Nome* by Angalo de Haberdasheri.

Let the eye of your imagination be a camera. . . .

This is the globe of the world, a glittering blue and white ball like the ornament on some unimaginable Christmas tree.

Find a continent. . . . *Focus.*

This is a continent, a jigsaw of yellows, greens, and browns.

Find a place. . . . *Focus.*

This is a bit of the continent, sticking out into the warmer sea to the southeast. Most of its inhabitants call it Florida.

Actually, they don't. Most of its inhabitants don't call it anything. They don't even know it exists. Most of them have six legs, and buzz. A lot of them have eight legs, and spend a lot of time in webs waiting for six-legged inhabitants to arrive for lunch. Many of the rest have four legs, and bark or moo or even lie in swamps pretending to be logs. In fact, only a tiny proportion of the inhabitants of Florida have two legs, and even most of *them* don't call it Florida. They just go tweet, and fly around a lot.

Mathematically, an almost insignificant number of living things in Florida call it Florida. But they're the ones who matter. At least, in their opinion. And their opinion is the one that matters. In their opinion.

Find a highway. . . . *Focus.* . . . Traffic swishing quietly through the soft warm rain . . . *focus* . . . high weeds on the bank . . . *focus* . . . grass moving in a way that isn't quite like grass moving in the wind . . . *Focus* . . . a pair of tiny eyes. . . .

Focus. . . . *Focus.* . . . *Focus.* . . . Click!

Masklin crept back through the grass to the nomes' camp, if that's what you could call a tiny dry space under a scrap of thrown-away plastic.

It had been hours since they'd run away from Grandson Richard, 39, as Gurder kept on putting it. The sun was rising behind the rain clouds.

They'd crossed a highway while there was no traffic, they'd blundered around in damp undergrowth, scurrying away from every chirp and mysterious croak, and finally they'd found the plastic. And they'd slept. Masklin stayed on guard for a while, but he wasn't certain what he was guarding against.

There was a positive side. The Thing had been listening to radio and television and had found the place the going-straight-up shuttles went from. It was only eighteen miles away. And they'd definitely made progress. They'd gone—oh, call it half a mile. And at least it was warm. Even the rain was warm. And the bacon, lettuce, and tomato sandwich was holding up.

But there were still almost eighteen miles to go.

"When did you say the launch is?" said Masklin.

"Four hours time," said the Thing.

"That means we'll have to travel at more than four miles an hour," said Angalo gloomily.

Masklin nodded. A nome, trying hard, could probably cover a mile and a half in an hour over open ground.

He hadn't given much thought to how they could get the Thing into space. If he'd thought about it at all, he'd imagined that they could find the shuttle plane and wedge the Thing on it somewhere. If possible maybe they could go, too, although he wasn't too sure about that. The Thing said it was cold in space, and there was no air.

"You could have asked Grandson Richard, 39, to help us!" said Gurder. "Why did you run away?"

"I don't know," said Masklin. "I suppose I thought we ought to be able to help ourselves."

"But you used the Truck. Nomes lived in the Store. You used the Concorde. You're eating human food."

Masklin was surprised. The Thing didn't often argue like that.

"That's different," he said.

"How?"

"They didn't know about us. We took what we wanted. We weren't given it. They think it's their world, Thing! They think everything in it belongs to them! They name everything and own everything! I looked up at him, and I thought, here's a human in a human's room, doing human things. How can he ever understand about nomes? How can he ever think tiny people are real people with real thoughts? I can't just let a human take over. Not just like that!"

The Thing blinked a few lights at him.

"We've come too far not to finish it ourselves," Masklin mumbled. He looked up at Gurder.

"Anyway, when it came to it, I didn't exactly see you rushing up, ready to shake him by the finger," he said.

"I was embarrassed. It's always embarrassing, meeting deities," said Gurder.

They hadn't been able to light a fire. Everything was too wet. Not that they needed a fire, it was just that a fire was more civilized. Someone had managed to light a fire there at some time, though, because there were still a few damp ashes.

"I wonder how things are back home?" said Angalo, after a while.

"All right, I expect," said Masklin.

"Do you really?"

"Well, more *hope* than expect, to tell the truth."

"I expect your Grimma's got everyone organized," said Angalo, trying to grin.

"She's not my Grimma," snapped Masklin.

"Isn't she? Whose is she, then?"

"She's . . ." Masklin hesitated. "Hers, I suppose," he said lamely.

"Oh. I thought the two of you were set to—" Angalo began.

"We're not. I told her we were going to get married, and all she could talk about was frogs," said Masklin.

"That's females for you," said Gurder. "Didn't I say that letting them learn to read was a bad idea? It overheats their brains."

"She said the most important thing in the world was little frogs living in a flower," Masklin went on, trying to listen to the voice of his own memory. He hadn't been listening very hard at the time. He'd been too angry.

"Sounds like you could boil a *kettle* on her head," said Angalo.

"It was something she'd read in a book, she said."

"My point exactly," said Gurder. "You know I never really agreed with letting everyone learn to read. It unsettles people."

Masklin looked gloomily at the rain.

"Come to think of it," he said, "It wasn't frogs exactly. It was the *idea* of frogs. She said there are these hills where it's hot and rains all the time, and in the rain forests there are these very tall trees and right in the top branches of the trees there are these like great big flowers called . . . bromeliads, I think, and water gets into the flowers and makes little pools and there's a type of frog that lays eggs in the pools and tadpoles hatch and grow into new frogs and these little frogs live their whole lives in the flowers right at the top of the trees and don't even know about the ground, and once you know the world is full of things like that, your life is never the same."

He took a deep breath.

"Something like that, anyway," he said.

Gurder looked at Angalo.

"Didn't understand *any* of it," he said.

"*It's a metaphor,*" said the Thing. No one paid it any attention.

Masklin scratched his ear. "It seemed to mean a lot to her," he said.

"*It's a metaphor,*" said the Thing.

"Women always want something," said Angalo. "My wife is always on about dresses."

"I'm sure he would have helped," said Gurder. "If we'd talked to him. He'd probably have given us a proper meal and, and—"

"Given us a home in a shoebox," said Masklin.

"And given us a home in a shoebox," said Gurder automatically. "No! I mean, maybe. I mean, why not? A decent hour's sleep for a change. And then we—"

"We'd be carried around in his pocket," said Masklin.

"Not necessarily. Not necessarily."

"We would. Because he's big and we're small."

"*Launch in three hours and fifty-seven minutes,*" said the Thing.

Their temporary camp overlooked a ditch. There didn't seem to be any winter in Florida, and the banks were thick with greenery.

Something like a flat plate with a spoon on the front sculled slowly past. The spoon stuck out of the water for a moment, looked at the nomes vaguely, and then dropped down again.

"What was that thing, Thing?" said Masklin.

The Thing extended one of its sensors.

"*A long-necked turtle.*"

"Oh."

The turtle swam peacefully away.

"Lucky, really," said Gurder.

"What?" said Angalo.

"Its having a long neck like that *and* being called a Long-Necked Turtle. It'd be really awkward having a name like that if it had a short neck."

"Launch in three hours and fifty-six minutes."

Masklin stood up.

"You know," said Angalo, "I really wish I could have read more of *The Spy with No Trousers*. It was getting exciting."

"Come on," he said. "Let's see if we can find a way."

Angalo, who had been sitting with his chin in his hands, gave him an odd look.

"What now?"

"We've come too far just to stop, haven't we?"

They pushed their way through the weeds. After a while a fallen log helped them across the ditch.

"Much greener here than at home, isn't it?" said Angalo.

Masklin pushed through a thick stand of leaves.

"Warmer too," said Gurder. "They've got the heating fixed here." *

---

* For generations the Store nomes had known that temperature was caused by air conditioning and the heating system; like many of them, Gurder never quite gave up certain habits of thinking.

"No one fixes heating Outside, it just happens," said Angalo.

"If I get old, this is the kind of place I'd like to live, if I had to live Outside," Gurder went on, ignoring him.

"It's a wildlife preserve," said the Thing.

Gurder looked shocked. "What? Like jam? Made of *animals?*"

"No. It is a place where animals can live unmolested."

"You're not allowed to hunt them, you mean?"

"Yes."

"You're not allowed to hunt anything, Masklin," said Gurder.

Masklin grunted.

There was something nagging at him. He couldn't quite put his finger on it. Probably it was to do with the animals after all.

"Apart from turtles with long necks," he said, "what other animals are there here, Thing?"

The Thing didn't answer for a moment. Then it said, *"I find mention of sea cows and alligators."*

Masklin tried to imagine what a sea cow looked like. But they didn't sound too bad. He'd met cows before. They were big and slow and didn't eat nomes, except by accident.

"What's an alligator?" he said.

The Thing told him.

"What?" said Masklin.

"What?" said Angalo.

"*What?*" said Gurder. He pulled his robe tightly around his legs.

"You idiot!" shouted Angalo.

"Me?" said Masklin hotly. "How should I know? How should I know? Is it my fault? Did I miss a sign at the airport saying 'Welcome to Floridia, home of large meat-eating reptiles up to twelve feet long'?"

They watched the grasses. A damp warm world inhabited by insects and turtles was suddenly a disguise for horrible terrors with huge teeth.

Something's watching us, Masklin thought. I can feel it.

The three nomes stood back-to-back. Masklin crouched down, slowly, and picked up a stone.

The grass moved.

"The Thing did say they don't all grow to twelve feet," said Angalo, in the silence.

"We were blundering around in the darkness!" said Gurder. "With things like that around!"

The grass moved again. It wasn't the wind that was moving it.

"Pull yourself together," muttered Angalo.

"If it *is* alligators," said Gurder, trying to look noble, "I shall show them how a nome can die with dignity."

"Please yourself," said Angalo, his eyes scanning the undergrowth. "I'm planning to show them how a nome can run away with speed."

The grasses parted.

A nome stepped out.

There was a crackle behind Masklin. His head spun around. Another nome stepped out.

And another.

And another.

Fifteen of them.

The three travelers swiveled like an animal with six legs and three heads.

It was the fire that I saw, Masklin told himself. We sat right down by the ashes of a fire, and I looked at them, and I didn't wonder who could have made them.

The strangers wore gray. They seemed to be all sizes. And every single one of them had a spear.

I wish I had mine, Masklin thought, trying to keep as many of the strangers as possible in his line of sight.

They weren't pointing their spears at him. The trouble was, they weren't exactly *not* pointing them, either.

Masklin told himself that it was very rare for a nome to kill another nome. In the Store it was considered bad manners, while Outside . . . well, there were so many other things that killed nomes in any case. Besides, it was wrong. There didn't have to be any other reasons.

He just had to hope that these nomes felt the same way.

"Do you know these people?" said Angalo.

"Me?" said Masklin. "Of course not. How could I?"

"They're Outsiders. I dunno, I suppose I thought all Outsiders would know each other."

"Never seen them before in my life," said Masklin.

"I *think*," said Angalo, slowly and deliberately, "that the leader is that old guy with the big nose and the topknot with a feather in it. What do you think?"

Masklin looked at the tall, thin old nome who was scowling at the three of them.

"He doesn't look as if he likes us very much."

"I don't like the look of him at *all*," said Angalo.

"Have you got any suggestions, Thing?" said Masklin.

"They are probably as frightened of you as you are of them."

"I doubt it," said Angalo.

"Tell them you will not harm them."

"I'd much rather they told me they're not going to harm *us*."

Masklin stepped forward, and raised his hands.

"We are peaceful," he said. "We don't want anyone to be hurt."

"Including us," said Angalo. "We really mean it."

Several of the strangers backed away and raised their spears.

"I've got my hands raised," said Masklin over his shoulder, "Why should they be so upset?"

"Because you're holding a large rock," said Angalo flatly. "I don't know about them, but if you walked toward me holding something like that *I'd* be pretty scared."

"I'm not sure I want to let go of it," said Masklin.

"Perhaps they don't understand us."

Gurder moved.

He hadn't said a word since the arrival of the new nomes. He'd just gone very pale.

Now some sort of internal timer had gone off. He gave a snort, leapt forward, and he bore down on Topknot like an enraged balloon.

"How *dare* you accost us, you—you *Outsider!*" he screamed.

Angalo put his hands over his eyes. Masklin got a firm hold on his rock.

"Er, Gurder . . ." he began.

Topknot backed away. The other nomes seemed puzzled by the small explosive figure that was suddenly among them. Gurder was in the grip of the kind of anger that is almost as good as armor.

Topknot screeched something back at Gurder.

"Don't you harangue me, you grubby heathen," said Gurder. "Do you think all these spears really frighten us?"

"Yes," whispered Angalo. He sidled closer to Masklin. "What's got into him?" he said.

Topknot shouted something at his nomes. A couple of them raised their spears, uncertainly. Several of the others appeared to argue.

"This is getting worse," said Angalo.

"Yes," said Masklin. "I think we should—"

A voice behind them snapped out a command. All the Floridians turned. So did Masklin.

Two nomes had come out of the grass. One was a boy. The other was a small, dumpy woman, the sort you'd cheerfully accept an apple pie from. Her hair was tied in a bun, and like Topknot's, it had a long gray feather stuck through it.

The Floridians looked sheepish. Topknot spoke at length. The woman said a couple of words. Topknot spread his arms above him and muttered something at the sky.

The woman walked around Masklin and Angalo as if they were items on display. When she looked Masklin up and down he caught her eye and thought: She looks like a little old lady, but she's in charge. If she doesn't like us, we're in a lot of trouble.

She reached up and took the stone out of his hand. He didn't resist.

Then she touched the Thing.

It spoke. What it said sounded very much like the words the woman had just used. She pulled her hand away sharply, and looked at the Thing with her head on one side. Then she stood back.

At another command the Floridians formed, not

a line, but a sort of *V* shape with the woman at the tip of it and the travelers inside it.

"Are we prisoners?" said Gurder, who had cooled off a bit.

"I don't think so," said Masklin. "Not exactly prisoners, yet."

The meal was some sort of a lizard. Masklin quite enjoyed it; it reminded him of his days as an Outsider. The other two ate it only because not eating it would be impolite, and it probably wasn't a good idea to be impolite to people who had spears when you didn't.

The Floridians watched them solemnly.

There were at least thirty of them, all wearing identical gray clothes. They looked quite like the Store nomes, except for being slightly darker and much skinnier. Many of them had large, impressive noses, which the Thing said was perfectly okay and all because of genetics.

The Thing was talking to them. Occasionally it would extend one of its sensors and use it to draw shapes in the dirt.

"Thing's probably telling them we-come-from-place-bilong-far-on-big-bird-that-doesn't-go-flap," said Angalo.

A lot of the time the Thing was simply repeating the woman's own words back at her.

Eventually Masklin couldn't stand it anymore.

"What's *happening*, Thing?" he said. "Why's the woman doing all the talking?"

"She is the leader of this group," said the Thing.

"A woman? Are you serious?"

"I am always serious. It's built in."

"Oh."

Angalo nudged Masklin. "If Grimma ever finds out, we're in *real* trouble," he said.

"Her name is Very-small-tree, or Shrub," the Thing went on.

"And you can understand her?" said Masklin.

"Gradually. Their language is very close to original nomish."

"What do you mean, original nomish?"

"The language your ancestors spoke."

Masklin shrugged. There was no point in trying to understand that now.

"Have you told her about us?" he said.

"Yes. She says—"

Topknot, who had been muttering to himself, stood up suddenly and spoke very sharply at great length, with a lot of pointing to the ground and to the sky.

The Thing flashed a few lights.

"He says you are trespassing on the land belonging to the Maker of Clouds. He says that is very bad. He said the Maker of Clouds will be very angry."

There was a general murmur of agreement from many of the nomes.

Shrub spoke to them sharply. Masklin stuck out a hand to stop Gurder from getting up.

"What does, er, Shrub think?" he said.

"I don't think she is very sympathetic to the topknot person. His name is Person-who-knows-what-the-Maker-of-Clouds-is-thinking."

"And what is the Maker of Clouds?"

"It's bad luck to say its true name. It made the ground and it is still making the sky. It—"

Topknot spoke again. He sounded angry.

We need to be friends with these people, Masklin thought. There has to be a way.

"The Maker of Clouds is"—Masklin thought hard—"a sort of Arnold Bros. (est. 1905)?"

"Yes," said the Thing.

"A real thing?"

"I think so. Are you prepared to take a risk?"

"What?"

"I think I know the identity of the Maker of Clouds. I think I know when it will make some more sky."

"What? When?" said Masklin.

"In three hours and ten minutes."

Masklin hesitated.

"Hold on a moment," he said, slowly, "that sounds like the same sort of time that—"

"Yes. All three of you, please get ready to run. I will now write the name of the Maker of Clouds."

"Why will we have to run?"

"They might get very angry. But we haven't time to waste."

The Thing extended a sensor. It wasn't intended as a writing implement, and the shapes it drew were angular and hard to read.

It scrawled four shapes in the dust.

The effect was instantaneous.

Topknot started to shout again. Some of the Floridians leapt to their feet. Masklin grabbed the other two travelers.

"I'm really going to thump that old nome in a minute," said Gurder. "How can anyone be so narrow-minded?"

Shrub sat silent while the row went on around her. Then she spoke, very loud but very calmly.

"She is telling them," said the Thing, *"that it is not wrong to write the name of the Maker of Clouds. It is often written by the Maker of Clouds itself. 'How famous the Maker of Clouds must be, that even these strangers know its name,' she says."*

That seemed to satisfy most of the nomes. Topknot started to grumble to himself.

Masklin relaxed a bit, and looked down at the figures in the sand.

"N . . . A . . . 8 . . . A?" he said.

"It's an S," said the Thing, *"Not an* 8."

"But you've only been talking to them for a little while!" said Angalo. "How can you know something like this?"

"Because I know how nomes think," said the Thing. *"You always believe what you read, and you've all got very literal minds. Very literal minds indeed."*

Six

Geese: A type of bird which is slower than the *Concorde,* and you don't get anything to eat. According to nomes who know them well, a goose is the most stupid bird there is, except for a duck. Geese spend a lot of time flying to other places. As a form of transport, the goose leaves a lot to be desired. If it weren't for the nomes telling them what to do, geese would just fly around lost and honking the whole time, if you want my scientific opinion.
—From *A Scientific Encyclopedia for the Enquiring Young Nome* by Angalo de Haberdasheri.

In the beginning, said Shrub, there was nothing but ground. NASA saw the emptiness above the ground, and decided to fill it with sky. It built a place in the middle of the world and sent up towers full of clouds. Sometimes they also carried stars because, at night, after one of the cloud towers had gone up, the nomes could sometimes see new stars moving across the sky.

The land around the cloud towers was NASA's special country. There were more animals there, and fewer humans. It was a pretty good place for nomes. Some of them believed that NASA had arranged it all for precisely that reason.

Shrub sat back.

"And does she believe that?" said Masklin. He looked across the clearing to where Gurder and Topknot were arguing. They couldn't understand what one another was saying, but they were still arguing.

The Thing translated.

Shrub laughed.

"She says, Days come, days go, who needs to believe anything? She sees things happen with her own eyes, and these are things she knows happen. Belief is a wonderful thing for those who need it, she says. But she knows this place belongs to NASA, because its name is on signs."

Angalo grinned. He was nearly in tears.

"They live right by the place the going-up jets go from and they think it's some sort of magic place!" he said.

"Isn't it?" said Masklin, almost to himself. "Anyway, it's no more strange than thinking the Store was the whole world. Thing, how do they watch the going-up jets? They're a long way away."

"Not far at all. Eighteen miles is not far at all, she says. She says they can be there in little more than an hour."

Shrub nodded at their astonishment, and then, without another word, stood up and walked away through the bushes. She signaled the nomes to follow her. Half a dozen Floridians trailed after their leader, making the shape of a *V* with her at the point.

After a few yards the greenery opened out again beside a small lake.

The nomes were used to large bodies of water. There were reservoirs near the airport. They were even used to ducks.

But the things paddling enthusiastically toward them were a lot bigger than ducks. Besides, ducks were like a lot of other animals and recognized in nomes the shape, if not the size, of humans and kept a safe distance away from them. They didn't come haring toward them as if the mere sight of them was the best thing that had happened all day.

Some of them were almost flying in their desire to get to the nomes.

Masklin looked around automatically for a weapon. Shrub grabbed his arm, shook her head, and said a couple of words.

"They're friendly," the Thing translated.

"They don't look it!"

"They're geese," said the Thing. *"Quite harmless,*

except to grass and minor organisms. They fly here for the winter."

The geese arrived with a bow wave that surged over the nomes' feet, and arched their necks down toward Shrub. She patted a couple of fearsome-looking beaks.

Masklin tried hard not to look like a minor organism.

"*They migrate here from colder climates,*" the Thing went on. "*They rely on the Floridians to pick the right course for them.*"

"Oh, good. That's—" Masklin stopped while his brain caught up with his mouth. "You're going to tell me they fly on them, right?"

"*Certainly. They travel with the geese. Incidentally, you have two hours and forty-one minutes to launch.*"

"I want to make it absolutely clear," said Angalo slowly, as a great feathery head explored the waterweeds a few inches away, "that if you're suggesting that we ride on a geese—"

"*A goose. One geese is a goose.*"

"You can think again. Or compute, or whatever it is you do."

"*You have a better suggestion, of course,*" said the Thing. If it had a face, it would have been sneering.

"Suggesting we don't ride on them strikes me as a whole lot better, yes," said Angalo.

"I dunno," said Masklin, who had been watching the geese speculatively. "I might be prepared to give it a try."

"The Floridians have developed a very interesting relationship with the geese," said the Thing. *"The geese provide the nomes with wings, and the nomes provide the geese with brains. They fly north to Canada in the summer, and back here for the winter. Geese like nomes. Geese that carry nomes are steered to better feeding grounds, and find that their nests get protected from rats and other creatures. Geese are bright enough to learn that geese with nomes around have a better life. And the nomes get free transport and a warm place to sleep. It's almost a symbiotic relationship, although, of course, they're not familiar with the term."*

"Aren't they? Silly old them," Angalo muttered.

"I don't understand you, Angalo," said Masklin. "You're mad for riding in machines with whirring bits of metal pushing them along, yet you're worried about sitting on a perfectly natural bird."

"That's because I don't understand how birds work," said Angalo. "I've never seen an exploded working diagram of a goose."

"The geese are the reason the Floridians have never had much to do with humans," the Thing continued. *"As I said, their language is almost original nomish."*

"Yes, and I still don't understand that," said Masklin. "I mean, nomes ought to speak the same language, yes?"

"No. You remember that I told you once that nomes

used to be able to talk to humans, and taught them languages?"

"Yes?" said Masklin.

"And then the humans changed the language, over hundreds of years. Nomes who lived near humans changed too. But the Floridians never had much to do with humans, so their form of the language is still very much as it used to be."

Shrub was watching them carefully. There was something about the way she was treating them that still seemed odd to Masklin. It wasn't that she hadn't been afraid of them, or aggressive, or unpleasant.

"She's not surprised," he said aloud. "She's interested, but she's not surprised. They were upset because we were *here*, not because we existed. *How many other nomes has she met?"*

The Thing had to translate.

It was a word that Masklin had only known for a year.

Thousands.

The leading tree frog was trying to wrestle with a new idea. It was very dimly aware that it needed a new type of thought.

There had been the world, with the pool in the middle and the petals around the edge. One.

But farther along the branch was another world. From here it looked tantalizingly like the flower they had left. One.

The leading frog sat in a clump of moss and swiveled each eye so that it could see both worlds at the same time. One there. And one *there*.

One. And one.

The frog's forehead bulged as it tried to get its mind around a new idea. One and one were one. But if you had one *here* and one *there* . . .

The other frogs watched in bewilderment as their leader's eyes whizzed around and around.

One here and one there couldn't be one. They were too far apart. You needed a word that meant both ones. You needed to say . . . you needed to say . . .

The frog's mouth widened. It grinned so broadly that both ends almost met behind its head.

It had worked it out.

. . . *mipmip* . . . *!* it said.

It meant: One. And One *More* One!

Gurder was still arguing with Topknot when they got back.

"How do they manage to keep it up? They don't understand what each other's saying!" said Angalo.

"Best way," said Masklin. "Gurder? We're ready to go. Come on."

Gurder looked up. He was very red in the face. The two of them were crouched either side of a mass of scrawled diagrams in the dirt.

"I need the Thing!" he said. "This idiot refuses to understand anything!"

"You won't win any arguments with him," said Masklin. "Shrub says he argues with all the other nomes they meet. He likes to."

"What other nomes?" said Gurder.

"There's nomes everywhere, Gurder. That's what Shrub says. There's other groups even in Floridia. And—and—and in Canadia, where the Floridians go in the summer. There were probably even other nomes back home! We just never found them!"

He pulled the Abbot to his feet.

"And we haven't got a lot of time left," he added.

"I'm not going up on one of those things!"

The geese gave Gurder a puzzled look, as if he were an unexpected frog in their waterweed.

"I'm not very happy about it either," said Masklin, "but Shrub's people do it all the time. You just snuggle down in the feathers and hang on."

"*Snuggle?*" shouted Gurder. "I've never snuggled in my life!"

"You rode on the Concorde," Angalo pointed out. "And that was built and driven by humans."

Gurder glared like someone who wasn't going to give in easily.

"Well, who built the geese?" he demanded.

Angalo grinned at Masklin, who said: "What? Dunno. Other geese, I expect."

"Geese? *Geese?* And what do *they* know about designing for air safety?"

"Listen," said Masklin, "They can take us all the way across this place. The Floridians fly thousands of miles on them. Thousands of miles, without even any smoked salmon or pink wobbly stuff. It's worth trying it for eighteen miles, isn't it?"

Gurder hesitated. Topknot muttered something. Gurder cleared his throat.

"Very well," he said haughtily. "I'm sure if this misguided individual is in the habit of flying on these things, I should have no difficulty whatsoever." He stared up at the gray shapes bobbing out in the lagoon. "Do the Floridians talk to the creatures?"

The Thing tried this on Shrub. She shook her head. No, she said, geese were quite stupid. Friendly but stupid. Why talk to something that couldn't talk back?

"Have you told her what we're doing?" said Masklin.

"No. She hasn't asked."

"How do we get on?"

Shrub stuck her fingers in her mouth and whistled.

Half a dozen geese waddled up the bank. Close up, they didn't look any smaller.

"I remember reading something about geese

once," said Gurder, in a sort of dreamy terror. "It said they could break a human's arm with a blow of their nose."

"Wing," said Angalo, looking up at the feathery gray bodies looming over him. "It was their wing."

"And it was swans that do that," said Masklin, weakly. "Geese are the ones you mustn't say boo to."

Gurder watched a long neck weave back and forth above him.

"Wouldn't dream of it," he said.

A long time after, when Masklin came to write the story of his life, he described the flight of the geese as the fastest, highest, and most terrifying of all.

People said, Hold on, that's not right. You said the plane went so fast that it left its sound behind, and so high up there was blue all around it.

And he said, That's the point. It went so fast you didn't know how fast it was going, it went so high you couldn't see how high it was. It was just something that happened. And the Concorde looked as though it was *meant* to fly. When it was on the ground it looked kind of lost.

The geese, on the other hand, looked as aerodynamic as a pillow. They didn't roll into the sky and sneer at the clouds like the plane did. No, they ran across the top of the water and hammered desperately at the air with their wings and then, just when it was obvious they weren't going to achieve anything, they suddenly did; the water dropped away, and there was just the slow creak of wings pulling the goose up into the sky.

Masklin would be the first to admit that he didn't understand about jets and engines and machines, so maybe that was why he didn't worry about traveling in them. But he thought he knew a thing or two about muscles, and the knowledge that it was only a couple of big muscles that were keeping him alive was not comforting.

Each traveler shared a goose with one of the Floridians. They didn't do any steering, as far as Masklin could see. That was all done by Shrub, who sat far out on the neck of the leading goose. He never found out how she steered. Maybe by orders in some language the geese and the geese nomes shared. Maybe by little movements. Maybe (according to Angalo) by some sort of Science. It was a mystery. But then—he told himself—Shrub probably wouldn't know how to drive a truck. She'd probably be very impressed, he told himself. That made him feel a bit better.

The ones behind Shrub's bird followed their leader in a perfect *V* shape.

Masklin buried himself in the feathers. It was comfortable, if a bit cold. Floridians, he learned later, had no difficulty sleeping on a flying goose. The mere thought made Masklin's hands sweat.

He peered out just long enough to see distant trees sweeping by much too fast, and stuck his head down again.

"How long have we got, Thing?" he said.

"I estimate arrival in the vicinity of the launch pad one hour from launch."

"I suppose there's absolutely no possibility that launches have anything to do with lunches?" said Masklin wistfully.

"No."

"Pity. Well—have you any suggestions about how we get on the machine?"

"That is almost impossible."

"I thought you'd say that."

"But you could put me on," the Thing added.

"Yes, but how? Tie you to the outside?"

"No. Get me close enough and I will do the rest."

"What rest?"

"Call the Ship."

"Yes, where *is* the Ship? I'm amazed satellites and things haven't bumped into it."

"It is waiting."

"You're a great help, sometimes."

"Thank you."

"That was meant to be sarcastic."

"I know."

There was a rustling beside Masklin and his Floridian co-rider pushed aside a feather. It was the boy he had seen with Shrub. He'd said nothing, but just stared at Masklin and the Thing. Now he grinned, and said a few words.

"*He wants to know if you feel sick.*"

"I feel fine," Masklin lied. "What's his name?"

"*His name is Pion. He is Shrub's oldest son.*"

Pion gave Masklin another encouraging grin.

"*He wants to know what it is like in a jet,*" said the Thing. "*He says it sounds exciting. They see them sometimes, but they keep away from them.*"

The goose canted sideways. Masklin tried to hang on with his toes as well as his fingers.

"*It must be much more exciting than geese, he says,*" said the Thing.

"Oh, I don't know," said Masklin weakly.

Landing was much worse than flying. It would have been better on water, Masklin was told later, but Shrub had brought them down on land. The geese didn't like that much. It meant that they had almost to stand on the air, flapping furiously, and then drop the last few inches.

Pion helped Masklin down onto the ground, which seemed to him to be moving from side to side. The other travelers tottered toward him through the throng of birds.

"The ground!" panted Angalo. "It was so close! No one seemed to mind!"

He sagged to his knees.

"And they made honking noises!" he said. "And kept swinging from side to side! And they're all knobbly under the feathers!"

Masklin flexed his arms to let the tension out.

The land around them didn't seem a lot different from the place they'd left, except that the vegetation was lower and Masklin couldn't see any water.

"*Shrub says that this is as close as the geese can go,*" the Thing said. "*It is too dangerous to go any farther.*"

Shrub nodded, and pointed to the horizon.

There was a white shape on it.

"That?" said Masklin.

"That's it?" said Angalo.

"*Yes.*"

"Doesn't look very big," said Gurder quietly.

"It's still quite a long way off," said Masklin.

"I can see helicopters," said Angalo. "No wonder Shrub didn't want to take the geese any closer."

"And we must be going," said Masklin. "We've got an hour, and I reckon that's barely enough. Er. We'd better say good-bye to Shrub. Can you explain, Thing? Tell her that—that we'll try to find her again. Afterward. If everything's all right. I suppose."

"If there is any afterward," Gurder added. He looked like a badly washed dishcloth.

Shrub nodded when the Thing had finished translating, and then pushed Pion forward.

The Thing told Masklin what she wanted.

"What? We can't take him with us!" said Masklin.

"*Young nomes in Shrub's people are encouraged to travel,*" said the Thing. "*Pion is only fourteen months old and already he has been to Alaska.*"

"Try to explain that we're not going to a Laska," said Masklin. "Try to make her understand that all sorts of things could happen to him!"

The Thing translated.

"*She says that is good. A growing boy should always seek out new experiences.*"

"What? Are you translating me properly?" said Masklin suspiciously.

"*Yes.*"

"Well, have you told her it's dangerous?"

"*Yes. She says that danger is what being alive is all about.*"

"But he could be killed!" Masklin shrieked.

"*Then he will go up into the sky and become a star.*"

"Is that what they believe?"

"*Yes. They believe that the operating system of a nome starts off as a goose. If it is a good goose, it becomes a nome. When a good nome dies, NASA takes it up into the sky and it becomes a star.*"

"What's an operating system?" said Masklin. This was religion. He always felt out of his depth with religion.

"*The thing inside you that tells you what you are,*" said the Thing.

"It means a soul," said Gurder wearily.

"Never heard such a lot of nonsense," said Angalo cheerfully. "At least, not since we were in the

Store and believed we came back as garden ornaments, eh?" He nudged Gurder in the ribs.

Instead of getting angry about this, Gurder just
looked even more despondent.

"Let the lad come if he likes," Angalo went on.
"He shows the right spirit. He reminds me of me
when I was like him."

*"His mother says that if he gets homesick he can al-
ways find a goose to bring him back,"* said the Thing.

Masklin opened his mouth to speak.

But there were times when you couldn't say
anything because there was nothing to say. If you
had to explain anything to someone else, then
there had to be something you were both sure of,
someplace to start, and Masklin wasn't sure that
there was anyplace like that around Shrub. He
wondered how big the world was to her. Probably
bigger than he could imagine. But it stopped at the
sky.

"Oh, all right," he said. "But we have to go right
away. No time for long tearful—"

Pion nodded to his mother and came and stood
by Masklin, who couldn't think of anything to say.
Even later on, when he understood the geese
nomes better, he never quite got used to the way
they cheerfully parted from one another. Dis-
tances didn't seem to mean much to them.

"Come on, then," he managed.

Gurder glowered at Topknot, who had insisted

on coming this far. "I really wish I could talk to that nome," he said.

"Shrub told me he's quite a decent nome, really," said Masklin. "He's just a bit set in his ways."

"Just like you," said Angalo.

"Me? I'm not—" Gurder began.

"Of course you're not," said Masklin, soothingly. "Now, let's go."

They jogged through scrub two or three times as high as they were.

"We'll never have time," Gurder panted.

"Save your breath for running," said Angalo.

"Do they have smoked salmon on shuttles?" said Gurder.

"Dunno," said Masklin, pushing his way through a particularly tough clump of grass.

"No, they don't," said Angalo authoritatively. "I remember reading about it in a book. They eat out of tubes."

The nomes ran in silence while they thought about this.

"What, toothpaste?" said Gurder, after a while.

"No, not toothpaste. Of course not toothpaste. I'm *sure* not toothpaste."

"Well, what else do you know that comes in tubes?"

Angalo thought about this.

"Glue?" he said, uncertainly.

"Doesn't sound like a good meal to me. Tooth-paste and glue?"

"The people who drive the space jets must like it. They were all smiling in the picture I saw," said Angalo.

"That wasn't smiling, that was probably just them trying to get their teeth apart," said Gurder.

"No, you've got it all wrong," Angalo decided, thinking fast. "They have to have their food in tubes because of gravity."

"What about gravity?"

"There isn't any."

"Any what?"

"Gravity. So everything floats around."

"What, in water?" said Gurder.

"No, in air. Because there's nothing to hold it on the plate, you see."

"Oh." Gurder nodded. "Is that where the glue comes in?"

Masklin knew that they could go on like this for hours. What these sounds mean, he thought, is: I am alive and so are you. And we're all very wor-ried that we might not be alive for much longer, so we'll just keep talking, because that's better than thinking.

It all looked better when it was days or weeks away, but now when it was—

"How long, Thing?"

"Forty minutes."

"We've got to have another rest! Gurder isn't running, he's just falling upright."

They collapsed in the shade of a bush. The shuttle didn't look much closer, but they could see plenty of other activity. There were more helicopters. According to Pion, who climbed up the bush, there were humans, much farther off.

"I need to sleep," said Angalo.

"Didn't you sleep on the goose?" said Masklin.

"Did *you*?"

Angalo stretched out in the shade.

"How are we going to get on the shuttle thing?" he said.

Masklin shrugged. "Well, the Thing says we don't have to get on it, we just have to put the Thing on it."

Angalo pushed himself up on his elbows. "You mean we don't get to ride on it? I was looking forward to that!"

"I don't think it's like the Truck, Angalo. I don't think they leave a window open for anyone to sneak in," said Masklin. "I think it'd take more than a lot of nomes and some string to fly it, anyway."

"You know, that was the best time of my life, when I drove the Truck," said Angalo dreamily. "When I think of all those months I lived in the Store, not even knowing about the Outside . . ."

Masklin waited politely. His head felt heavy.

"Well?" he said.

"Well, what?"

"What happens when you think of all those months in the Store not knowing about the Outside?"

"It just seems like a waste."

Pion curled up and started to snore. Angalo yawned.

They hadn't slept for hours. Nomes slept mainly at night, but needed catnaps to get through the long day. Even Masklin was nodding.

"Thing?" he remembered to say, "wake me up in ten minutes, will you?"

Seven

Satellites: They are in *space* and stay there by going so fast that they never stay in one place long enough to fall down. *Televisions* are bounced off them.

> —From *A Scientific Encyclopedia for the Enquiring Young Nome* by Angalo de Haberdasheri.

It wasn't the Thing that woke Masklin up. It was Gurder.

Masklin lay with his eyes half closed, listening. Gurder was talking to the Thing in a low voice.

"I believed in the Store," he said, "and then I found out it was just a—a sort of thing built by humans. And I thought Grandson Richard, 39, was some special person and he turned out to be a human who sings when he wets himself—"

"Takes a shower!"

"And now there's thousands of nomes in the world! Thousands! Believing all sorts of things!

That stupid Topknot person believes that the going-up shuttles make the sky. Do you know what I
thought when I heard that? I thought, if he'd been
the one arriving in my world instead of the other
way around, he'd have thought I was just as stupid! I *am* just as stupid! . . . Thing?"

"*I was maintaining a tactful silence.*"

"Angalo believes in silly machinery and Masklin believes in, oh, I don't know. Space. Or not
believing in things. And it all works for them. I
try to believe in *important* things, and they don't
last for five minutes. Where's the fairness in that?"

"*Only another tactful and understanding silence suf-
fices at this point.*"

"I just wanted to make some *sense* out of life."

"*This is a commendable aim.*"

"I mean, what is the *truth* of everything?"

There was a pause. Then the Thing said: "*I re-
call your conversation with Masklin about the origin of
nomes. You wanted to ask me. I can answer now. I was
made. I know this is true. I know that I am a thing made
of metal and plastic, but also that I am something which
lives inside that metal and plastic. It is impossible for me
not to be absolutely certain of it. This is a great comfort.
As to nomes, I have data that says nomes originated on
another world and came here thousands of years ago.
This may be true. It may not be true. I am not in a
position to judge.*"

"I knew where I was, back in the Store," said
Gurder, half to himself. "And even in the quarry

it wasn't too bad. I had a proper job. I was important to people. How can I go back now, knowing that everything I believed about the Store and Arnold Bros. (est. 1905) and Grandson Richard, 39, is just . . . is just an *opinion*?"

"I cannot advise. I am sorry."

Masklin decided it was a diplomatic time to wake up. He made a grunting noise just to be sure that Gurder heard him.

The Abbot was very red in the face.

"I couldn't sleep," he said shortly.

Masklin stood up.

"How long, Thing?"

"Twenty-seven minutes."

"Why didn't you wake me up!"

"I wished you to be refreshed."

"But it's still a long way off. We'll never get you onto it in time. Wake up, you." Masklin prodded Angalo with his foot. "Come on, we'll have to run. Where's Pion? Oh, there you are. Come *on*, Gurder."

They jogged on through the scrub. In the distance, there was the low mournful howl of sirens.

"You're cutting it really fine, Masklin," said Angalo.

"Faster! Run faster!"

Now that they were closer, Masklin could see the shuttle. It was quite high up. There didn't seem to be anything useful at ground level.

"I hope you've got a good plan, Thing," he

panted, as the four of them dodged between the bushes, "because I'll never be able to get you all the way up there."

"*Do not worry. We are nearly close enough.*"

"What do you mean? It's still a long way off!"

"*It is close enough for me to get on.*"

"What is it going to do? Take a flying leap?" said Angalo.

"*Put me down.*"

Masklin obediently put the black box on the ground. It extended a few of its probes, which swung around slowly for a while and then pointed toward the going-up jet.

"What are you playing at?" said Masklin. "This is wasting *time!*"

Gurder laughed, although not in a very happy way.

"I know what it's doing," he said. "It's sending itself onto the shuttle. Right, Thing?"

"*I am transmitting an instruction subset to the computer on the communications satellite,*" said the Thing.

The nomes said nothing.

"*Or to put it another way . . . yes, I am turning the satellite computer into a part of me. Although not a very intelligent one.*"

"Can you really do that?" said Angalo.

"*Certainly.*"

"Wow. And you won't miss the bit you're sending?"

"*No. Because it will not leave me.*"

"You're sending it and keeping it at the same time?"

"*Yes.*"

Angalo looked at Masklin.

"Did you understand any of that?" he demanded.

"I did," said Gurder. "The Thing's saying it's not just a machine, it's a sort of—a sort of collection of electric thoughts that lives in a machine. I think."

Lights flickered around on top of the Thing.

"Does it take a long time to do?" said Masklin.

"*Yes. Please do not take up vital communication power at this point.*"

"I think he means he doesn't want us to talk to him," said Gurder. "He's concentrating."

"It," said Angalo. "It's an it. And it made us run all the way here just so we can hurry up and wait."

"It probably has to be close up to do . . . whatever it is it's doing," said Masklin.

"How long's it going to take?" said Angalo. "It seems ages since it was twenty-seven minutes ago."

"Twenty-seven minutes at least," said Gurder.

"Yeah. Maybe more."

Pion pulled at Masklin's arm, pointed to the looming white shape with his other hand, and rattled off a long sentence in Floridian, or if the Thing was right, nearly original nomish.

"I can't understand you without the Thing," said Masklin. "Sorry."

"No speaka da goose-oh," said Angalo.

A look of panic spread across the boy's face. He shouted this time, and tugged harder.

"I think he doesn't want to be near the going-up jets when they start up," said Angalo. "He's probably afraid of the noise. Don't . . . like . . . the . . . noise, right?" he said.

Pion nodded furiously.

"They didn't sound too bad at the airport," said Angalo. "More of a rumble. I expect they might frighten unsophisticated people."

"I don't think Shrub's people are particularly unsophisticated," said Masklin thoughtfully. He looked up at the white tower. It had seemed a long way away, but in some ways it might be quite close.

Really very close.

"How safe do you think it is here?" he said. "When it goes up, I mean."

"Oh, come *on*," said Angalo. "The Thing wouldn't have let us come right here if it wasn't safe for nomes."

"Sure, sure," said Masklin. "Right. You're right. Silly to dwell on it, really."

Pion turned and ran.

The other three looked back at the shuttle. Lights moved in complicated patterns on the top of the Thing.

Somewhere another siren sounded. There was a sensation of power, as though the biggest spring in the world was being wound up.

When Masklin spoke, the other two seemed to hear him speak their own thoughts.

"Exactly how good," he said, very slowly, "do you think the Thing is at judging how close nomes can stand to a going-up jet when it goes up? I mean, how much experience has it got, do you think?"

They looked at one another.

"Maybe we should back off a little bit?" Gurder suggested.

They turned and walked away.

Then each one of them couldn't help noticing that the others seemed to be walking faster and faster.

Faster and faster.

Then, as one nome, they gave up and ran for it, fighting their way through the scrub and grass, skidding on stones, elbows going up and down like pistons. Gurder, who was normally out of breath at anything above walking pace, bounded along like a balloon.

"Have . . . *you* . . . any—any . . . idea . . . how—how . . . close—" Angalo panted.

The sound behind them started like a hiss, like the whole world taking a deep breath. Then it turned into . . . not noise, but something more like an invisible hammer that smacked into both ears at once.

Eight

Space: There are two types: a) something containing nothing and b) nothing containing everything. It is what you have left when you haven't got anything else. There is no air or gravity, which is what holds people onto things. If there weren't space, everything would be in one place. It is designed to be a place for *satellites, shuttles, planets,* and *the Ship.*

—From *A Scientific Encyclopedia for the Enquiring Young Nome* by Angalo de Haberdasheri.

After some time, when the ground had stopped shaking, the nomes picked themselves up and stared blearily at one another.

"   !" said Gurder.

"What?" said Masklin. His own voice sounded a long way away, and muffled.

"   ?" said Gurder.

"   ?" said Angalo.

"   ?"

"What? I can't hear you! Can you hear *me*?"

"   ?"

Masklin saw Gurder's lips move. He pointed to his own ears and shook his head.

"We've gone deaf!"

"   ?"

"   ?"

"Deaf, I said." Masklin looked up.

Smoke billowed overhead and out of it, rising fast even to a nome's high-speed senses, was a long, growing cloud tipped with fire. The noise dropped to something merely very loud and then, very quickly, disappeared.

Masklin stuck a finger in his ear and wiggled it around.

The absence of sound was replaced by the terrible hiss of silence.

"Anyone listening?" he ventured. "Anyone hearing me?"

"That," said Angalo, his voice sounding blurred and unnaturally calm, "was pretty loud. I don't reckon many things come much louder."

Masklin nodded. He felt as though he'd been pounded hard by something.

"You know about these things," he said weakly. "Humans ride on them, do they?"

"Oh, yes. Right at the top."

"No one makes them do it?"

"Er. I don't think so," said Angalo. "I think the book said a lot of them want to do it."

"They *want* to do it?"

Angalo shrugged. "That's what it said."

There was only a distant dot now, at the end of a widening white cloud of smoke.

Masklin watched it.

We must be *mad*, he thought. We're tiny and it's a big world and we never stop to learn enough about where we are before we go somewhere else. At least back when I lived in a hole I knew everything there was to know about living in a hole, and now it's a year later and I'm at a place so far away I don't even know how far away it is, watching something I don't understand go to a place so far up there is no down. And I can't go back. I've got to go right on to the end of whatever all this is, because I can't go back. I can't even stop.

So *that's* what Grimma meant about the frogs. Once you know things, you're a different person. You can't help it.

He looked back down. Something was missing. The Thing.

He ran back the way they'd come.

The little black box was where he'd left it. The rods had withdrawn into it, and there weren't any lights.

"Thing?" he said uncertainly.

One red light came on faintly. Masklin suddenly felt cold, despite the heat around him.

"Are you all right?" he said.

The light flickered.

"Too quick. Used too much pow . . ." it said.

"Pow?" said Masklin. He tried hard not to wonder why the word hadn't been much more than a growl.

The light dimmed.

"Thing? Thing?" He tapped gently on the box. "Did it work? Is the Ship coming? What do we do now? Wake up! *Thing?*"

The light went out.

Masklin picked the Thing up and turned it over and over in his hands.

"Thing?"

Masklin and Gurder hurried up, with Pion behind them.

"Did it work?" said Angalo. "Can't see any Ship yet."

Masklin turned his face toward them.

"The Thing's stopped," he said.

"Stopped?"

"All the lights have gone out!"

"Well, what does that mean?" Angalo started to look panicky.

"I don't know!"

"Is it dead?" said Gurder.

"It *can't* die! It's existed for thousands of years!"

Gurder shook his head. "Sounds like a good reason for dying," he said.

"But it's a—a *Thing*."

Angalo sat down with his arms around his knees.

"Did it say if it got everything sorted out? When's the Ship coming?"

"Listen, don't you care? It's run out of pow!"

"Pow?"

"It must mean electricity. It kind of sucks it out of wires and stuff. I think it can store it for a while too. And now it must have run out."

They looked at the black box. It had spent thousands of years being handed down from nome to nome without ever saying a word or lighting a light. It had only woken up again when it had been brought into the Store, near electricity.

"It looks creepy, sitting there doing nothing," said Angalo.

"Can't we find it some electricity?" said Gurder.

"Around here? There isn't any!" Angalo snapped. "We're in the middle of nowhere!"

Masklin stood up and gazed around. It was just possible to see some buildings in the distance. There was a movement of vehicles around them.

"What about the *Ship*?" said Angalo. "Is it on its way?"

"I don't know!"

"How will it find us?"

"I don't know!"

"Who's driving it?"

"I don't—" Masklin stopped in horror. "No

one! I mean, who *could* be driving it? There hasn't been anyone on it for thousands of years!"

"Who was going to bring it here, then?"

"I don't know! The Thing, maybe?"

"You mean it's on its way and no one's driving it?"

"Yes! No! I don't know!"

Angalo squinted up at the blue sky.

"Oh, wow," he said glumly.

"We need to find some electricity for the Thing," said Masklin. "Even if it's managed to summon the Ship, the Ship will still need to be told where we are."

"*If* it summoned the Ship," said Gurder. "It might have run out of pow before it had time."

"We can't be sure," said Masklin. "Anyway, we must help the Thing. I hate to see it like that."

Pion, who had disappeared into the scrub, came back dragging a lizard.

"Ah," said Gurder, without any enthusiasm. "Here comes lunch."

"If the Thing were talking, we could tell Pion you can get awfully tired of lizard, in time," said Angalo.

"In about two seconds," said Gurder.

"Come on," said Masklin, wearily. "Let's go and find some shade and think up another plan."

"Oh, a plan," Gurder said, as if that was worse than lizard. "I like plans."

They ate—not very well—and lay back watching the sky. The brief sleep on the way hadn't been enough. It was easy to doze.

"I must say these Floridians have got it all worked out," said Gurder lazily. "It's cold back home and here they've got the heating turned up just right."

"I keep telling you, it's not the heating," said Angalo, straining his eyes for any sign of a descending Ship. "And the wind isn't the air conditioning, either. It's the sun that makes you warm."

"I thought that was just for lighting," said Gurder.

"And it's where all the heat comes from," said Angalo. "I read it in a book. It's a great ball of fire bigger than the world."

Gurder eyed the sun suspiciously.

"Oh, yes?" he said. "What keeps it up?"

"Nothing. It's just kind of *there.*"

Gurder squinted at the sun again.

"Is this generally known?" he said.

"I suppose so. It was in the book."

"For anyone to read? I call that irresponsible. That's the sort of thing that can really upset people."

"There are thousands of suns up there, Masklin says."

Gurder sniffed. "Yes, he's told me. It's called the glaxie, or something. Personally, I'm against it."

Angalo chuckled.

"I don't see what's so funny," said Gurder coldly.

"Tell him, Masklin," said Angalo.

"It's all very well for you," Gurder muttered. "You just want to drive things fast. *I* want to make sense of them. Maybe there *are* thousands of suns, but *why?*"

"Can't see that it matters," said Angalo lazily.

"It's the only thing that does matter. Tell him, Masklin."

They both looked at Masklin.

At least, where Masklin had been sitting.

He'd gone.

Beyond the top of the sky was the place the Thing had called the universe. It contained, according to the Thing, everything and nothing. And there was very little everything and more nothing than anyone could imagine.

For example, it was often said that the sky was full of stars. It was untrue. The sky was full of sky. There were unlimited amounts of sky and, really, by comparison, very few stars.

It was amazing, therefore, that they made such an impression.

Thousands of them looked down now as something round and shiny drifted around the Earth.

It had Arnsat-1 painted on its side, which was a bit of a waste of paint since stars can't read.

It unfolded a silver dish.

It should then have turned to face the planet below it, ready to beam down old movies and new news.

It didn't. It had new orders.

Little puffs of gas jetted out as it turned around and searched the sky for a new target.

By the time it had found it, a lot of people in the old movies and new news business were shouting very angrily at one another on telephones, and some of them were feverishly trying to give it new instructions.

But that didn't matter, because it wasn't listening anymore.

Masklin galloped through the scrub.

They'd argue and bicker, he thought. I've got to do this quickly. I don't think we've got a lot of time.

It was the first time he'd been really alone since the days back when he'd lived in a hole and had to go out hunting by himself because there was no one else.

Had it been better then? At least it had been simpler. You just had to try to eat without being eaten. Just getting through the day was a triumph. Everything had been bad, but at least it had been a kind of understandable, nome-sized badness.

In those days the world ended at the highway on one side and the woods beyond the field at the other side. Now it had no kind of boundaries at all, and more problems than he knew what to do with.

But at least he knew where to find electricity.

You found it near buildings with humans in them.

The scrub ahead of Masklin opened out onto a track.

He turned onto it, and ran faster. Go along any track, and you'd find humans on it somewhere.

There were footsteps behind him. He turned around, and saw Pion. The young Floridian gave him a worried smile.

"Go away!" Masklin said. "Go on! Go! Go back! Why are you following me? Go away!"

Pion looked hurt. He pointed up the track and said something.

"I don't understand!" shouted Masklin.

Pion stuck a hand high above his head, palm downward.

"Humans?" Masklin guessed. "Yes. I know. I know what I'm doing. Go back!"

Pion said something else.

Masklin lifted up the Thing. "Talking box no go," he said helplessly. "Good grief, why should I have to speak like this? You must be at least as intelligent as me. Go on, go away. Go back to the others."

He turned and ran. He looked back briefly, and saw Pion watching him.

How *much* time have I got? he wondered. Thing

once told me the Ship flies very fast. Maybe it could be here any minute. Maybe it's not coming at all.

He saw figures looming over the scrub. Yes, follow any track, and sooner or later you find humans. They get everywhere.

Yes, maybe the Ship isn't coming at all.

If it isn't, he thought, then what I'm going to do now is probably the most stupid thing any nome has ever done anywhere in the total history of nomekind.

He stepped out into a circle of gravel. A small truck was parked in it, with the name of the Floridian god NASA painted on the side. Close by, a couple of humans were bent over a piece of machinery on a tripod.

They didn't notice Masklin. He walked closer, his heart thumping.

He put down the Thing.

We used to talk, he said. Well, maybe it's time to try again.

He cupped his hands around his mouth.

He tried to shout as clearly and as slowly as possible.

"Hey, there! You! Hu—mans!"

"He did what?" shouted Angalo.

Pion ran through his pantomime of gestures again.

"*Talked* to *humans*?" said Angalo. "Went in a thing with *wheels*?"

"I thought I heard a truck engine," said Gurder.

Angalo pounded a fist into his palm.

"He was worried about the Thing," he said. "He wanted to find it some electricity!"

"But we must be miles from any buildings!" said Gurder.

"Not the way Masklin's going!" Angalo snarled.

"I *knew* it would come to this!" Gurder moaned. "Showing ourselves to humans! We never used to do that sort of thing in the Store! What are we going to *do*?"

Masklin thought, Up to now, it's not too bad.

The humans hadn't really known what to do about him. They'd even backed away! And then one of them had rushed to the truck and talked into a machine on a string. Probably some sort of telephone, Masklin thought knowledgeably.

When he hadn't moved, one of the humans had fetched a box out of the back of the truck and crept toward him as if expecting Masklin to explode. In fact, when he waved, the human jumped back clumsily.

The other human said something, and the box was cautiously put down on the gravel a few feet from Masklin.

Then both humans watched him expectantly.

He kept smiling, to put them at their ease, and

climbed into the box. Then he gave them another wave.

One of the humans reached down gingerly and picked up the box, lifting it up in the air as though Masklin was something very rare and delicate. He was carried to the truck. The human got in, and still holding the box with exaggerated care, placed it on its knees. A radio crackled with deep human voices.

Well, no going back now. Knowing that, Masklin very nearly relaxed. Perhaps it was best to look at it as just another step along life's sidewalk.

They kept staring at him as if they didn't believe what they were seeing.

The truck lurched off. After a while it turned onto a concrete road, where another truck was waiting. A human got out, spoke to the driver of Masklin's truck, laughed in a slow human way, looked down at Masklin, and stopped laughing very suddenly.

It almost ran back to its own truck and started speaking into another telephone.

I knew this would happen, Masklin thought. They don't know what to do with a real nome. Amazing.

But just so long as they take me somewhere where there's the right kind of electricity.

Dorcas, the engineer, had once tried to explain electricity to Masklin, but without much success because Dorcas wasn't too certain about it, either.

There seemed to be two kinds, straight and wiggly. The straight kind was very boring and stayed in batteries. The wiggly kind was found in wires in the walls and things, and somehow the Thing could steal some of it if it was close enough. Dorcas used to talk about wiggly electricity in the same tone of voice Gurder used for talking about Arnold Bros. (est. 1905). He'd tried to study it back in the Store. If it was put into freezers it made things cold, but if the same electricity went into an oven it made things hot, so how did it *know*?

Dorcas used to talk, Masklin thought. I said "used to." I hope he *still* does.

He felt light-headed and oddly optimistic. Part of him was saying: That's because if you for one second think seriously about the position you've put yourself in, you'll panic.

Keep smiling.

The truck purred along the road, with the other truck following it. Masklin saw a third truck rattle down a side road and pull in behind them. There were a lot of humans on it, and most of them were watching the skies.

They didn't stop at the nearest building, but drove on to a bigger one with many more vehicles outside. More humans were waiting for them.

One of them opened the truck door, doing it very slowly even for a human.

The human carrying Masklin got out of the truck.

Masklin looked up at dozens of staring faces. He could see every eyeball, every nostril. Every one of them looked worried. At least, every eyeball did. The nostrils just looked like nostrils.

They were worried about *him*.

Keep smiling.

He stared back up at them, and still almost giggling with repressed panic, said, "Can I help you, gentlemen?"

Nine

Science: A way of finding things out and then making them work. There is a lot more Science than you think.

    —From *A Scientific Encyclopedia for the Enquiring Young Nome* by Angalo de Haberdasheri.

Gurder, Angalo, and Pion sat under a bush. It gave them a bit of shade. The cloud of gloom over them was almost as big.

"We'll never even get home without the Thing," said Gurder.

"Then we'll get him out," said Angalo.

"That'll take forever!"

"Yeah? Well, that's nearly as long as we've got here, if we can't get home." Angalo had found a pebble that was almost the right shape to attach to a twig with strips torn off his coat; he'd never seen a stone ax in his life, but he had a definite feeling that there were useful things that could be done with a stone tied to the end of a stick.

"I wish you'd stop fiddling with that thing," Gurder said. "What's the big plan, then? Us against the whole of Floridia?"

"Not necessarily. You needn't come."

"Calm down, Mr. To-the-rescue. One idiot's enough."

"I don't hear you coming up with any better ideas." Angalo swished the ax through the air once or twice.

"I haven't got any."

A small red light started to flash on the Thing.

After a while, a small square hole opened up and there was a tiny whirring sound as the Thing extended a little lens on a stick. This turned around slowly.

Then the Thing spoke.

"Where," it asked, *"is this place?"*

It tilted the lens up and there was a pause while it surveyed the face of the human looking down at it.

"And why?" it added.

"I'm not sure," said Masklin. "We're in a room in a big building. The humans haven't hurt me. I think one of them has been trying to talk to me."

"We appear to be in some sort of glass box," said the Thing.

"They even gave me a little bed," said Masklin.

"And I think the thing over there is some kind of lavatory, but *look*, what about the Ship?"

"I expect it is on its way," said the Thing calmly.

"Expect? *Expect?* You mean you don't know?"

"Many things can go wrong. If they have gone right, the Ship will be here soon."

"If they don't, I'm stuck here for life!" said Masklin bitterly. "I came here because of you, you know."

"Yes. I know. Thank you."

Masklin relaxed a bit.

"They're being quite kind," he said. He thought about this. "At least, I think so," he added. "It's hard to tell."

He looked through the transparent wall. A lot of humans had been in to look at him in the last few minutes. He wasn't quite certain whether he was an honored visitor or a prisoner, or maybe something in between.

"It seemed the only hope at the time," he said lamely.

"I am monitoring communications."

"You're always doing that."

"A lot of them are about you. All kinds of experts are rushing here to have a look at you."

"What kind of experts? Experts in nomes?"

"Experts in talking to creatures from other worlds. Humans haven't met anyone from another world, but they've still got experts in talking to them."

"All this had better work," said Masklin soberly. "Humans really know about nomes now."

"*But not what nomes are. They think you have just arrived.*"

"Well, that's true."

"*Not arrived here. Arrived on the planet. Arrived from the stars.*"

"But we've been here for thousands of years! We *live* here!"

"*Humans find it a lot easier, really, to believe in little people from the sky than little people from the Earth. They would prefer to think of little green men than leprechauns.*"

Masklin's brow wrinkled. "I didn't understand any of that," he said.

"*Don't worry about it. It doesn't matter.*" The Thing let its lens swivel around to see more of the room.

"*Very nice. Very scientific,*" it said.

Then it focused on a wide plastic tray next to Masklin.

"*What is that?*"

"Oh, fruit and nuts and meat and stuff," said Masklin. "I think they've been watching me to see what I eat. I think these are quite bright humans, Thing. I pointed to my mouth and they understood I was hungry."

"*Ah,*" said the Thing. "*Take me to your larder.*"

"Pardon?"

"*I will explain. I have told you that I monitor communications?*"

"All the time."

"*There is a joke, that is, a humorous anecdote or story, known to humans. It concerns a ship from another world landing on this planet, and strange creatures get out and say to a gas pump, garbage can, slot-machine, or similar mechanical device, 'Take me to your leader.' I surmise this is because they are unaware of the shape of humans. I have substituted the similar word 'larder,' referring to a place where food is stored. This is a humorous pun, or play on words, for hilarious effect.*"

It paused.

"Oh," said Masklin. He thought about it. "These would be the little green men you mentioned?"

"*Very—wait a moment. Wait a moment.*"

"What? What?" said Masklin urgently.

"*I can hear the Ship.*"

Masklin listened as hard as he could.

"I can't hear a thing," he said.

"*Not sound. Radio.*"

"Where is it? Where is it, Thing? You've always said the Ship's up there, but *where*?"

The remaining tree frogs crouched among the moss to escape the heat of the afternoon sun.

Low in the eastern sky was a sliver of white.

It would be nice to think that the tree frogs had legends about it. It would be nice to think that they thought the sun and moon were distant flowers—a yellow one by day, a white one by night. It would be nice to think they had legends about them, and said that when a good frog died its soul would go to the big flowers in the sky.

The trouble is that it's *frogs* we're talking about here. Their name for the sun was . . . mipmip. . . . Their name for the moon was . . . mipmip. . . . Their name was *everything* was . . . mipmip . . . and when you're stuck with a vocabulary of one word it's pretty hard to have legends about anything at all.

The leading frog, however, was dimly aware that there was something wrong with the moon.

It was growing brighter.

"We left the Ship on the *moon?*" said Masklin. "Why?"

"That's what your ancestors decided to do," said the Thing. *"So they could keep an eye on it, I assume."*

Masklin's face lit up slowly, like clouds at sunrise.

"You know," he said, excitedly, "Right back before all this, right back when we used to live in the old hole, I used to sit out at nights and watch the moon. Perhaps in my blood I really knew that, up there—"

"No, what you were experiencing was probably primitive superstition," said the Thing.

Masklin deflated. "Oh. Sorry."

"And now, please be quiet. The Ship is feeling lost and wants to be told what to do. It has just woken up after fifteen thousand years."

"I'm not very good at mornings myself," Masklin said.

There is no sound on the moon, but this doesn't matter, because there is no one to hear anything. Sound would just be a waste.

But there is light.

Fine moondust billowed high across the ancient plains of the moon's dark crescent, expanding in boiling clouds that went high enough to catch the rays of the sun. They glittered.

Down below, something was digging itself out.

"We left it in a *hole?*" said Masklin.

Lights rippled back and forth across all surfaces of the Thing.

"Don't say that's why you always lived in holes," it said. *"Other nomes don't live in holes."*

"No, that's true," said Masklin. "I ought to stop thinking only about the—"

He suddenly went quiet. He stared out of the glass tank, where a human was trying to interest him in marks on a blackboard.

"You've got to stop it," he said. "Right now. Stop the Ship. We've got it all wrong. Thing, we can't go! It doesn't belong to just us! We can't take the Ship!"

* * *

The three nomes 'lurking near the shuttle launching place watched the sky. As the sun neared the horizon the moon sparkled like a Christmas decoration.

"It must be caused by the Ship!" said Angalo. "It must be!" He beamed at the others. "That's it, then. It's on its way!"

"I never thought it would work." Gurder said.

Angalo slapped Pion on the back, and pointed.

"See that, my lad?" he said. "That's the Ship, that is! Ours!"

Gurder rubbed his chin, and nodded thoughtfully at Pion.

"Yes," he said, "That's right. Ours."

"Masklin says there's all kinds of stuff up there," said Angalo dreamily. "And masses of space. That's what space is well known for, lots of space. Masklin said the Ship goes faster than light goes, which is probably wrong, otherwise how'd you see anything? You'd turn the lights on and all the light would drop backward out of the room. But it's pretty fast."

Gurder looked back at the sky again. Something at the back of his mind was pushing its way to the front, and giving him a curious gray feeling.

"Our Ship," he said. "The one that brought nomes here."

"Yeah, that's right," said Angalo, hardly hearing him.

"And it'll take us all back," Gurder went on.

"That's what Masklin said, and—"

"All nomes," said Gurder. His voice was as flat and heavy as a sheet of lead.

"Sure. Why not? I expect I'll soon work out how to drive it back to the quarry, and we can pick them all up. And Pion here, of course."

"What about Pion's people?" said Gurder.

"Oh, they can come too," said Angalo expansively. "There's probably even room for their geese!"

"And the others?"

Angalo looked surprised. "What others?"

"Shrub said there were lots of other groups of nomes. Everywhere."

Angalo looked blank. "Oh, them. Well, I don't know about them. But we *need* the Ship. You know what it's been like ever since we left the Store."

"But if we take the Ship away, what will *they* have if they need it?"

Masklin had just asked the same question.

The Thing said, "*0100110101010111010101001-0110101110010.*"

"What did you say?"

The Thing sounded tetchy. "*If I lose concentration, there might not be a Ship for anyone,*" it said. "*I am sending fifteen thousand instructions per second.*"

Masklin said nothing.

"*That's a lot of instructions,*" the Thing added.

"By rights the Ship must belong to all the nomes in the world," said Masklin.

"*010011001010010010—*"

"Oh, shut up and tell me when the Ship is going to get here."

"*0101011001 . . . Which do you want me to do? . . . 01001100 . . .*"

"What?"

"*I can shut up or I can tell you when the Ship is going to arrive. I can't do both.*"

"Please tell me when the Ship is going to arrive," said Masklin patiently, "and then shut up."

"*Four minutes.*"

"Four minutes!"

"*I could be three seconds off,*" said the Thing. "*But I calculate it as four minutes. Only now it's three minutes thirty-eight seconds. It'll be three minutes and thirty-seven seconds any second now—*"

"I can't hang around in here if it's coming that soon!" said Masklin, all thoughts of his duty to the nomes of the world temporarily forgotten. "How can I get out? This thing's got a lid on."

"*Do you want me to shut up first, or get you out and then shut up?*" said the Thing.

"Please!"

"*Have the humans seen you move?*" said the Thing.

"What do you mean?"

"*Do they know how fast you can run?*"

"I don't know," said Masklin. "I suppose not."

"Get ready to run, then. But first, put your hands over your ears."

Masklin thought it would be best to obey. The Thing could be deliberately infuriating at times, but it didn't pay to ignore its advice.

Lights on the Thing made a brief star-shaped pattern.

It started to wail. The sound went up and then went beyond Masklin's hearing. He could feel it even with his hands over his ears; it seemed to be making unpleasant bubbles in his head.

He opened his mouth to shout at the Thing, and the walls exploded. One moment there was glass, and the next there were bits of glass, drifting out like a jigsaw puzzle where every piece had suddenly decided it wanted some personal space. The lid slid down, almost hitting him.

"Now, pick me up and run," ordered the Thing, before the shards had spilled across the table.

Humans around the room were turning to look in that slow, clumsy way humans had.

Masklin grabbed the Thing and took off across the polished surface.

"Down," he said. "We're high up, how do we get down?" He looked around desperately. There was some sort of machine at the other end of the table, covered with little dials and lights. He'd watched one of the humans using it.

"Wires," he said, "There's always wires!"

He skidded around, dodged easily around a giant hand as it tried to grab him, and hared along the table.

"I'll have to throw you over," he panted. "I can't carry you down!"

"I'll be all right."

Masklin slid to a stop by the table edge and threw the Thing down. There *were* wires running down toward the floor. He leapt for one, swung around madly, and then half fell and half slid down it.

Humans were lurching toward him from everywhere. He picked up the Thing again, hugging it to his chest, and darted forward. There was a foot —brown shoe, dark blue sock. He zigged. There were two more feet—black shoes, black socks. And they were about to trip over the first foot.

He zagged.

There were more feet, and hands reaching vainly down. Masklin was a blur, dodging and weaving between feet that could flatten him.

And then there was nothing but open floor.

Somewhere an alarm sounded, its shrill note sounding deep and awesome to Masklin.

"Head for the door," suggested the Thing.

"But more humans'll be coming in," hissed Masklin.

"That's good, because we're going out."

Masklin reached the door just as it opened. A gap of a few inches appeared, with more feet behind it.

There wasn't any time to think. Masklin ran over the shoe, jumped down on the other side, and ran on.

"Where now? Where now?"

"Outside."

"Which way is that?"

"Every way."

"Thank you very much!"

Doors were opening all along the corridor. Humans were coming out. The problem was not evading capture—it would take a very alert human even to see a nome running at full speed, let alone catch one—but simply avoiding being trodden on by accident.

"Why don't they have mouse holes? Every building should have mouse holes!" Masklin moaned.

A boot stamped down an inch away. He jumped.

The corridor was filling with humans. Another alarm started to sound.

"Why's all this happening? I can't be causing all this! There can't be all this trouble over just one nome!"

"It's the Ship. They have seen the Ship."

A shoe almost awarded Masklin the prize for the most perfectly flattened nome in Florida. As it was, he almost ran into it.

Unlike most shoes, it had a name on it. It was a Crucial Street Drifter with Real Rubber Soul,

Pat'd. The sock above it looked as though it could be a Hi-style Odorprufe, made of Guaranteed 85% Polyputheketlon, the most expensive sock in the world.

Masklin looked farther up. Beyond the great sweep of blue trouser and the distant clouds of sweater was a beard.

It was Grandson Richard, 39.

Just when you thought there was no one watching over nomes, the universe went and tried to prove you wrong.

Masklin took a standing jump and landed on the trouser leg, just as the foot moved. It was the safest place. Humans didn't often tread on other humans.

The foot took a step and came down again. Masklin swung backward and forward, trying to pull himself up the rough cloth. There was a seam an inch away. He managed to grab it; the stitches gave a better handhold.

Grandson Richard, 39, was in a crush of people all heading the same way. Several other humans banged into him, almost jarring Masklin loose. He kicked his boots off and tried to grip with his toes.

There was a slow thumping as Grandson Richard's feet hit the ground.

Masklin reached a pocket, got a decent foothold, and climbed on. A bulky label helped him up to the belt. Masklin was used to labels in the Store, but this was pretty big even by big label standards. It was covered in lettering and had been riveted to the trousers, as if Grandson Richard, 39, were some sort of machine.

" 'Grossbergers Hagglers, the First Name in Jeans,' " he read. "And there's lots of stuff about how good they are, and pictures of cows and things. Why d'you think he wants labels all over himself?"

"Perhaps if he hasn't got labels, he doesn't know what his clothes are," said the Thing.

"Good point. He'd probably put his shoes on his head."

Masklin glanced back at the label as he grabbed the sweater.

"It says here that these jeans won a Gold Medal in the Chicago Exhibition in 1910," he said. "They've certainly lasted well."

Humans were streaming out of the building.

The sweater was much easier to climb. Masklin hauled himself up quickly. Grandson Richard, 39, had quite long hair, which also helped when it was time to climb up onto the shoulder.

A doorframe passed briefly overhead, and then the deep blue of the sky.

"How long, Thing?" Masklin asked. Grandson Richard's ear was only a few inches away.

"Forty-three seconds."

The humans spilled out of the wide concrete space in front of the building. Some more hurried out of the building, carrying machinery. They kept running into one another because they were all staring at the sky.

Another group was clustered around one human who was looking very worried.

"What's going on, Thing?" Masklin whispered.

"The human in the middle of the group is the most important one here. It came to watch the shuttle launch. Now all the others are telling it that it's got to be the one to welcome the Ship."

"That's a bit of cheek. It's not *their* Ship."

"Yes, but they think it's coming to talk to them."

"Why should they think that?"

"Because they think they're the most important creatures on the planet."

"Hah!"

"Amazing, isn't it?" said the Thing.

"Everyone knows nomes are more important," said Masklin. "At least . . . every nome does." He thought about this for a moment, and shook his head. "So that's the head human, is it? Is it some sort of extra wise one, or something?"

"I don't think so. The other humans around it are trying to explain to it what a planet is."

"Doesn't it know?"

"Many humans don't. Mistervicepresident is one of them. 001010011000."

"You're talking to the Ship again?"

"Yes. Six seconds."

"It's really coming?"

"Yes."

· *152* ·

Ten

Gravity: This is not properly understood, but it is what makes small things, like nomes, stick to big things, like planets. Because of *Science*, this happens whether you know about gravity or not. Which goes to show that Science is happening all the time.

—From *A Scientific Encyclopedia for the Enquiring Young Nome* by Angalo de Haberdasheri.

Angalo looked around.

"Gurder, come *on.*"

Gurder leaned against a tuft of grass and fought to get his breath back.

"It's no good," he wheezed. "What are you thinking of? We can't fight humans alone!"

"We've got Pion. And this is a pretty good ax."

"Oh, that's really going to scare them. A stone ax. If you had two axes I expect they'd give in right away."

Angalo swung it backward and forward. It had a comforting feel.

"You've got to try," he said simply. "Come on, Pion. What are you watching? Geese?"

Pion was staring at the sky.

"There's a dot up there," said Gurder, squinting.

"It's probably a bird," said Angalo.

"Doesn't look like a bird."

"Then it's a plane."

"Doesn't look like a plane."

Now all three of them were staring upward, their upturned faces forming a triangle.

There was a black dot up there.

"You don't think he actually *managed* it, do you?" said Angalo, uncertainly.

What had been a dot was now a small dark circle.

"It's not moving, though," said Gurder.

"It's not moving sideways, anyway," said Angalo, still speaking very slowly. "It's moving more sort of down."

What had been a small dark circle was a larger dark circle, with just a suspicion of smoke or steam around its edges.

"It might be some sort of weather," said Angalo. "You know—special Floridian weather?"

"Oh, yeah? One great big hailstone, right? It's the Ship! Coming for us!"

It was a lot bigger now, and yet, and yet . . . still a very long way off.

"If it could come for us just a little way away I wouldn't mind," Gurder quavered. "I wouldn't mind walking a little way."

"Yeah," said Angalo, beginning to look desperate. "It's not so much *coming* as, as . . ."

"*Dropping,*" said Gurder.

He looked at Angalo.

"Shall we run?" he said.

"It's got to be worth a try," said Angalo.

"Where shall we run to?"

"Let's just follow Pion, shall we? He started running a while ago."

Masklin would be the first to admit that he wasn't too familiar with forms of transport, but what they all seemed to have in common was a front, which was in front, and a back, which wasn't. The whole point was that the front was where they went forward from.

The thing dropping out of the sky was a disc— just a top connected to a bottom, with edges around the sides. It didn't make any noise, but it seemed to be impressing the humans no end.

"That's it?" he said.

"*Yes.*"

"Oh."

And then things seemed to come into focus.

The Ship wasn't big. It was so big, it needed a

new word. It wasn't dropping through the thin wisps of cloud up there, it was simply pushing them aside. Just when you thought you'd got some idea of the size, a cloud would stream past and the perspective would come back. There had to be a special word for something as big as that.

"Is it going to crash?" he whispered.

"*I shall land it on the scrub,*" said the Thing. "*I don't want to frighten the humans.*"

"Run!"

"What do you think I'm doing?"

"It's still right above us!"

"I'm running! I'm running! I can't run any faster!"

A shadow fell across the three running nomes.

"All the way to Floridia to be squashed under our own Ship," moaned Angalo. "You never really believed in it, did you? Well, now you're going to believe in it really hard!"

The shadow deepened. They could see it racing across the ground ahead of them—gray around the edges, spreading into the darkness of night. Their own private night.

"The others are still out there somewhere," said Masklin.

"*Ah,*" said the Thing. "*I forgot.*"

"You're not suppose to forget things like that!"

"I've been very busy lately. I can't think of everything. Just nearly everything."

"Just don't squash anyone!"

"I shall stop it before it lands. Don't worry."

The humans were all talking at once. Some of them had started to run toward the falling Ship. Some were running away from it.

Masklin risked a glance at Grandson Richard's face. It was watching the Ship with a strange, rapt expression.

As Masklin stared, the big eyes swiveled slowly sideways. The head turned around. Grandson Richard, 39, stared down at the nome on his shoulder.

For the second time, the human saw him. And this time, there was nowhere to run.

Masklin rapped the Thing on its lid.

"Can you slow my voice down?" he said quickly. An amazed expression was forming on the human's face.

"What do you mean?"

"I mean you just repeat what I say, but slowed down. And louder. So it—so he can understand it?"

"You want to communicate? *With a* human?"

"Yes! Can you do it?"

"I strongly advise against it! It could be very dangerous!"

Masklin clenched his fists. "Compared to what, Thing? Compared to what? How much more dangerous than *not* communicating, Thing? Do it! Right now! Tell him . . . tell him we're not trying to hurt any humans! Right now! I can see his hand moving already! Do it!" He held the box right up to Grandson Richard's ear.

The Thing started to speak in the low, slow tones of human speech.

It seemed to go on for a long time.

The human's expression froze.

"What did you say? What did you say?" said Masklin.

"I said, If he harms you in any way I shall explode and blow his head off," said the Thing.

"You didn't!"

"I did."

"You call that communicating?"

"Yes. I call it very effective communicating."

"But it's a dreadful thing to say! Anyway . . . you never told me you could explode!"

"I can't. But he doesn't know that. He's only human," said the Thing.

The Ship slowed its fall and drifted down across the scrubland until it met its own shadow. Beside it, the tower where the shuttle had been launched looked like a pin alongside a very large black plate.

"You landed it on the ground! I told you not to!" said Masklin.

"It's not on the ground. It is floating just above the ground."

"It looks as though it's on the ground to me!"

"It is floating just above it," repeated the Thing patiently.

Grandson Richard was looking down the length of his nose at Masklin. He looked puzzled.

"What makes it float?" Masklin demanded.

The Thing told him.

"Auntie who? Who's she? There are relatives on board?"

"Not auntie. Anti. Antigravity."

"But there's no flames or smoke!"

"Flames and smoke are not essential."

Vehicles were screaming toward the bulk of the Ship.

"Um. Exactly *how* far off the ground did you stop it?" Masklin inquired.

"Four inches seemed adequate."

Angalo lay with his face pressed into the sandy soil.

To his amazement, he was still alive. Or at least, if he was dead, then he was still able to think. Perhaps he *was* dead, and this was wherever you went afterward.

It seemed pretty much like where he'd been before.

Let's see, now. He'd looked up at the great thing dropping out of the sky right toward his head, and had flung himself down expecting at any second to become just a little greasy mark in a great big hole.

No, he probably hadn't died. He'd have remembered something important like that.

"Gurder?" he ventured.

"Is that you?" said Gurder's voice.

"I hope so. Pion?"

"Pion!" said Pion, somewhere in the darkness.

Angalo pushed himself up onto his hands and knees.

"Any idea where we are?" he said.

"In the Ship?" suggested Gurder.

"Don't think so," said Angalo. "There's soil here, and grass and stuff."

"Then where did the Ship go? Why's it all dark?"

Angalo brushed the dirt off his coat. "Dunno. Maybe . . . maybe it missed us. Maybe we were knocked out, and now it's nighttime?"

"I can see a bit of light around the horizon," said Gurder. "That's not right, is it? That's not how nights are supposed to be."

Angalo looked around. There *was* a line of light in the distance. And there was also a strange sound, so quiet that you could miss it but that, once you had noticed it, also seemed to fill up the world.

He stood up to get a better view.

There was a faint thump.

"Ouch!"

Angalo reached up to rub his head. His hand

touched metal. Crouching a little, he risked turning his head to see what it was he'd hit.

He got very thoughtful for a while.

Then he said, "Gurder, you're going to find this amazingly hard to believe."

"This time," said Masklin to the Thing, "I want you to translate *exactly*, do you understand? Don't try to frighten him!"

Humans had surrounded the Ship. At least, they were trying to surround it, but you'd need an awful lot of humans to surround something the size of the Ship. So they were just surrounding it in places.

More trucks were arriving, many of them with sirens blaring. Grandson Richard, 39, had been left standing by himself, watching his own shoulder nervously.

"Besides, we owe him something," said Masklin. "We used his satellite. And we stole things."

"You said you wanted to do it your way. No help from humans, you said," said the Thing.

"It's different now. There is the Ship," said Masklin. "We've made it. We're not begging anymore."

"May I point out that you're sitting on his shoulder, not him on yours," said the Thing.

"Never mind that," said Masklin. "Tell it—I mean, ask him to walk toward the Ship. And say 'please.' And say that we don't want anyone to get hurt. Including me," he added.

Grandson Richard's reply seemed to take a long time. But he did start to walk toward the crowds around the Ship.

"What did he say?" said Masklin, hanging on tightly to the sweater.

"I don't believe it," said the Thing.

"He doesn't believe me?"

"He said his grandfather always talked about the little people, but he never believed it until now. He said, Are you like the ones in the old Store?"

Masklin's mouth dropped open. Grandson Richard, 39, was watching him intently.

"Tell him yes," Masklin croaked.

"Very well. But I do not think it'll be a good idea."

The Thing boomed. Grandson Richard rumbled a reply.

"He says his grandfather made jokes about little people in the Store," said the Thing. *"He used to say they brought him luck."*

Masklin felt the horrible sensation in his stomach that meant the world was changing again, just when he thought he understood it.

"Did his grandfather ever see a nome?" he said.

"He says no. But he says that when his grandfather and his grandfather's brother were starting the Store, and stayed late every night to do the office work, they used to hear sounds in the walls and they used to tell each other there were little Store people. It was a sort of joke.

*He says that when he was small, his grandfather used to
tell him about little people who came out at night to play
with the toys."*

"But the Store nomes never did things like
that!" said Masklin.

"I didn't say the stories were true."

The Ship was a lot closer now. There didn't
seem to be any doors or windows anywhere. It
was as featureless as an egg.

Masklin's mind was in turmoil. He'd always believed that humans were quite intelligent. After
all, nomes were very intelligent. Rats were quite
intelligent. And foxes were intelligent, more or
less. There ought to be enough intelligence slosh-
ing around in the world for humans to have some
too. But this was something more than intelligence.

He remembered a book called *Gulliver's Travels.*
It had been a big surprise to the nomes. There had
never been an island of small people. He was certain of that. It was a—a—a made-up thing. There
had been lots of books in the Store that were like
that. They'd caused no end of problems for the
nomes. For some reason, humans needed things
that weren't true.

They never really thought nomes existed, he
thought, but they wanted to believe that we did.

"Tell him," he said, "tell him I must get into the
Ship."

Grandson Richard, 39, whispered. It was like listening to a gale.

"He says there are too many people."

"Why are all the humans around it?" said Masklin, bewildered. "Why aren't they frightened?"

Grandson Richard's reply was another gale.

"He says they think some creatures from another world will come out and talk to them."

"Why?"

"I don't know," said the Thing. *"Perhaps they don't want to be alone."*

"But there's no one in it! It's *our* Ship—" Masklin began.

There was a wail. The crowd put their hands over their ears.

Lights appeared on the darkness of the Ship. They twinkled all over the hull in patterns that raced backward and forward and disappeared. There was another wail.

"There *isn't* anyone in it, is there?" said Masklin. "No nomes were left on it in hibernation or anything?"

High up on the Ship a square hole opened. There was a whiffling noise and a beam of red light shot out and set fire to a patch of scrub several hundred yards away.

People started to run.

The Ship rose a few feet, wobbling alarmingly. It drifted sideways a little. Then it went straight up so fast that it was just a blur and jerked to a

halt high over the crowd. And then it turned over.
And then it went on its edge for a while.

It floated back down again and landed, more or
less. That is, one side touched the ground and the
other rested on the air, on nothing.

The Ship spoke, loudly.

To the humans it must have sounded like a high-
pitched chattering.

What it actually said was: "Sorry! Sorry! Is this
a microphone? Can't find the button that opens
the door. . . . Let's try this one. . . ."

Another square hole opened. Brilliant blue light
flooded out.

The voice boomed out across the country again.

"Got it!" There was the distorted *thud-thud* of
someone not certain if their microphone was
working, and tapping it experimentally. "Masklin,
are you out there?"

"That's Angalo!" said Masklin. "No one else
drives like that! Thing, tell Grandson Richard, 39,
I must get on the Ship! Please!"

The human nodded.

Humans were milling around the base of the
Ship. The doorway was too high up for them to
reach.

With Masklin hanging on grimly, Grandson
Richard, 39, pushed his way through the throng.

The ship wailed again.

"Er," came Angalo's hugely amplified voice, apparently talking to someone else, "I'm not sure

about this switch, but maybe it's. . . . Certainly I'm going to press it, why shouldn't I press it? It's next to the door one, it must be safe. Look, shut up. . . ."

A silver ramp wound out of the doorway. It looked big enough for humans.

"See? See?" said Angalo's voice.

"Thing, can you speak to Angalo?" said Masklin. "Can you tell him I'm out here, trying to get to the Ship?"

"No. He appears to be randomly pressing buttons. It is to be hoped that he does not press the wrong ones."

"I thought you could tell the Ship what to do!" said Masklin.

The Thing managed to sound shocked. *"Not when a nome is in it,"* it said. *"I can't tell it not to do what a nome tells it to do. That's what being a machine is all about."*

Grandson Richard, 39, was shoving his way through the pushing, shouting mass of humans, but it was hard going.

Masklin sighed.

"Ask Grandson Richard, 39, to put me down," he said. Then he added, "And say thank you. Say it . . . it would have been nice to talk more."

The Thing did the translation.

Grandson Richard, 39, looked surprised. The Thing spoke again. Then he reached up a hand toward Masklin.

If he had to make a list of terrifying moments,

Masklin would have put this one at the top. He'd faced foxes, he'd helped to drive the Truck, he'd flown on a goose—but none of them were half so bad as letting a human being actually touch him. The huge whorled fingers uncurled and passed on either side of his waist. He shut his eyes.

Angalo's booming voice said, "Masklin? Masklin? If anything bad's happened to you, there's going to be *trouble.*"

Grandson Richard's finger gripped Masklin lightly, as though the human was holding something very fragile. Masklin felt himself being slowly lowered toward the ground.

He opened his eyes. There was a forest of human legs around him.

He looked up into Grandson Richard's huge face, and trying to make his voice as deep and slow as possible, said the last word any nome said to any human:

"Good-bye."

Then he ran through the maze of feet.

Several humans with official-looking trousers and big boots were standing at the bottom of the ramp. Masklin scurried between them and ran on upward.

Ahead of him blue light shone out of the open hatchway. As he ran he saw two dots appear on the lip of the entrance.

The ramp was long. Masklin hadn't slept for hours. He wished he'd got some sleep on the bed when the humans were studying; it had looked quite comfortable.

Suddenly, all his legs wanted to do was go somewhere close and lie down.

He staggered to the top of the ramp and the dots became the heads of Gurder and Pion. They reached out and pulled him into the Ship.

He turned around and looked down into a sea of human faces, below him. He'd never looked down on a human before.

They probably couldn't even see him. They're waiting for the little green men, he thought.

"Are you all right?" said Gurder urgently. "Did they do anything to you?"

"I'm fine, I'm fine," murmured Masklin. "No one hurt me."

"You look dreadful."

"We should have talked to them, Gurder," said Masklin. "They *need* us."

"Are you *sure* you're all right?" said Gurder, peering anxiously at him.

Masklin's head felt full of cotton wool. "You know how you believed in Arnold Bros. (est. 1905)?" he managed to say.

"Yes," said Gurder.

Masklin gave him a mad, triumphant grin.

"Well, he believed in you too! How about that?"

And Masklin folded up, very gently.

Eleven

The Ship: The machine used by nomes to leave Earth. We don't yet know everything about it, but since it was built by nomes using *Science,* we will.
—From *A Scientific Encyclopedia for the Enquiring Young Nome* by Angalo de Haberdasheri.

The ramp wound in. The doorway shut. The Ship rose in the air until it was high above the buildings.

And it stayed there, while the sun set.

The humans below tried shining colored lights at it, and playing tunes at it, and eventually just speaking to it in every language known to humans.

It didn't seem to take any notice.

Masklin woke up.

He was on a very uncomfortable bed. It was all soft. He hated lying on anything softer than the ground. The Store nomes liked sleeping on fancy bits of carpet, but Masklin's bed had been a bit of wood. He'd used a piece of rag for a cover and thought that was luxury.

He sat up and looked around the room. It was fairly empty. There was just the bed, a table, and a chair.

A table and a chair.

In the Store, the nomes had made their furniture out of matchboxes and cotton reels; the nomes living Outside didn't even know what furniture *was*.

This looked rather like human furniture, but it was nome-sized.

Masklin got up and padded across the metal floor to the door. Nome-sized, again. A doorway made by nomes for nomes to walk through.

It led into a corridor, lined with doors. There was an old feel about it. It wasn't dirty or dusty. It just felt like somewhere that had been absolutely clean for a very, very long time.

Something purred toward him. It was a small black box, rather like the Thing, mounted on little treads. A little revolving brush on the front was sweeping dust into a slot. At least, if there had been any dust it would have been sweeping it. Masklin wondered how many times it had industriously cleaned this corridor, while it waited for nomes to come back.

It bumped into his foot, beeped at him, and then

bustled off in the opposite direction. Masklin followed it.

After a while he passed another one. It was moving along the ceiling with a faint clicking noise, cleaning it.

He turned the corner, and almost walked into Gurder.

"You're up!"

"Yes," said Masklin. "Er. We're on the Ship, right?

"It's amazing . . . !" Gurder began. He looked wild-eyed, and his hair was sticking up at all angles.

"I'm sure it is," said Masklin reassuringly.

"But there's all these . . . and there's great big . . . and there are these *huge* . . . and you'd never believe how wide . . . and there's so much . . ." Gurder's voice trailed off. He looked like a nome who would have to learn new words before he could describe things.

"It's too big!" he blurted out. He grabbed Masklin's arm.

"Come on," he said, and half ran along the corridor.

"How did you get on?" said Masklin, trying to keep up.

"It was amazing! Angalo touched this panel thing and it just moved aside and then we were inside and there was an elevator thing and then we were in this great big room with a seat and

Angalo sat down and all these lights came on and he started pressing buttons and moving things!"

"Didn't you try to stop him?"

Gurder rolled his eyes. "You know Angalo and machines," he said. "But the Thing is trying to get him to be sensible. Otherwise we'd be crashing into stars by now," he added gloomily.

He led the way through another arch into— well, it had to be a room. It was inside the Ship. It was just as well he knew that, Masklin thought, because otherwise he'd think it was Outside. It stretched away, as big as one of the departments in the Store.

Vast screens and complicated-looking panels covered the walls. Most of them were dark. Shadowy gloom stretched away in every direction, except for a little puddle of light in the very center of the room.

It illuminated Angalo in a big padded chair. He had the Thing in front of him, on a sloping metal board studded with switches. He had obviously been arguing with it. When Masklin walked up, he glared at him and said, "It won't do what I tell it!"

The Thing looked as small and black and square as it could.

"He wants to drive the Ship," it said.

"You're a machine! You *have* to do what you're told!" snapped Angalo.

"I'm an intelligent *machine, and I don't want to end*

up very flat at the bottom of a deep hole," said the Thing. *"You can't pilot the Ship yet."*

"How do you know? You won't let me try! I drove the Truck, didn't I? It wasn't my fault all those trees and streetlights and things got in the way," he added, after catching Masklin's eye.

"I expect the Ship is more difficult," said Masklin diplomatically.

"But I'm learning about it all the time," said Angalo. "It's easy. All the buttons have got little pictures on them. Look . . ."

He pressed a button.

One of the big screens lit up, showing the crowds outside the Ship.

"They've been waiting there for ages," said Gurder.

"What do they want?" said Angalo.

"Search me," said Gurder. "Who knows what humans want?"

Masklin stared at the throng below the ship.

"They've been trying all sorts of stuff," said Angalo. "Flashing lights and music and stuff like that. And radio, too, the Thing says."

"Haven't you tried talking back to them?" said Masklin.

"No. Haven't got anything to say." said Angalo. He rapped on the Thing with his knuckles. "Right, Mr. Clever? If I'm not going to do the driving, who is?"

"Me."

"How?"

"There is a slot by the seat."

"I see it. It's the same size as you."

"Put me in it."

Angalo shrugged, and picked up the Thing. It slid smoothly into the floor until only the top of it was showing.

"Look, er," said Angalo, "can't I do something? Operate the windshield wipers or something? I'd feel like a twerp sitting here doing nothing."

The Thing didn't seem to hear him. Its light flickered on and off for a moment, as if it were making itself comfortable in a mechanical kind of way. Then it said, in a much deeper voice than it had ever used before:

"RIGHT."

Lights came on all over the Ship. They spread out from the Thing like a tide; panels lit up like little skies full of stars, big lights in the ceiling flickered on, there was a distant banging and fizzing as electricity was woken up, and the air began to smell of thunderstorms.

"It's like the Store at Christmas Fayre," said Gurder.

"Science!" breathed Angalo.

"ALL SYSTEMS IN WORKING ORDER," boomed the Thing. *"NAME OUR DESTINATION."*

"What?" said Masklin. "And don't shout."

"Where are we going?" said the Thing. *"You have to name our destination."*

"It's got a name already. It's called the quarry, isn't it?" said Masklin.

"Where is it?" said the Thing.

"It's . . ." Masklin waved an arm vaguely. "Well, it's over that way somewhere."

"Which way?"

"How should I know? How many ways are there?"

"Thing, are you telling us you don't know the way back to the quarry?" said Gurder.

"That is correct."

"We're lost?"

"No. I know exactly what planet we're on," said the Thing.

"We can't be lost," said Gurder. "We're here. We know where we are. We just don't know where we aren't."

"Can't you find the quarry if you go up high enough?" said Angalo. "You ought to be able to see it, if you go up high enough."

"Very well."

"Can I do it?" said Angalo. "Please?"

"Press down with your left foot and pull back on the green lever, then," said the Thing.

There wasn't so much a noise as a change in the type of silence. Masklin thought he felt heavy for a moment, but then the sensation passed.

The picture in the screen got smaller.

"Now, this is what I call proper flying," said

Angalo, happily. "With real Science. No noise and none of that stupid flapping."

"Yes, where's Pion?" said Masklin.

"He wandered off," said Gurder. "I think he was going to get something to eat."

"On a machine that no nome has been on for fifteen thousand years?" said Masklin.

Gurder shrugged. "Well, maybe there's something at the back of a cupboard somewhere," he said. "I want a word with you, Masklin."

"Yes?"

Gurder moved closely and glanced over his shoulder at Angalo, who was lying back in the control seat with a look of dreamy contentment on his face.

He lowered his voice.

"We shouldn't be doing this," he said. "I know it's a dreadful thing to say, after all we've been through. But this isn't just *our* Ship. It belongs to all nomes, everywhere."

He looked relieved when Masklin nodded.

"A year ago you didn't even believe there were any other nomes anywhere," Masklin said.

Gurder looked sheepish. "Yes. Well. That was then. This is now. I don't know what I believe in anymore, except that there must be thousands of nomes out there we don't know about. There might even be other nomes living in Stores! We're just the lucky ones who had the Thing. So if we take the Ship away, there won't be any hope for them."

"I know, I know," said Masklin wretchedly. "But what can we do? *We* need the Ship right now. Anyway, how could we find these other nomes?"

"We've got the Ship!" said Gurder.

Masklin waved a hand at the screen, where the landscape was spreading out and becoming misty.

"It'd take forever to find nomes down there. You couldn't do it even with the Ship. You'd have to be on the ground. Nomes keep hidden! You nomes in the Store didn't know about my people, and we lived a few miles away. We'd never have found Pion's people except by accident. Besides"—he couldn't resist prodding Gurder gently—"there's a bigger problem too. You know what we nomes are like. Those other nomes probably wouldn't even *believe* in the Ship."

He was immediately sorry he'd said that. Gurder looked more unhappy than he'd ever seen him.

"That's true," the Abbot said. "I wouldn't have believed it. I'm not sure I believe it now, and I'm *in* it."

"Maybe, when we've found somewhere to live, we can send the Ship back and collect any other nomes we can find," Masklin hazarded. "I'm sure Angalo would enjoy that."

Gurder's shoulders began to shake. For a moment Masklin thought the nome was laughing, and then he saw the tears rolling down the Abbot's face.

"Um," he said, not knowing what else to say.

Gurder turned away. "I'm sorry," he muttered. "It's just that there's so much . . . changing. Why can't things stay the same for five minutes? Every time I get the hang of an idea it suddenly turns into something different and *I* turn into a fool! All I want is something real to believe in! Where's the harm in that?"

"I think you just have to have a flexible mind," said Masklin, knowing even as he said the words that this probably wasn't going to be a lot of help.

"Flexible? Flexible? My mind's got so flexible I could pull it out of my ears and tie it under my chin!" snapped Gurder. "And it hasn't done me a whole lot of good, let me tell you! I'd have done better just believing everything I was taught when I was young! At least I'd be wrong only once! This way I'm wrong all the time!"

He stamped away down one of the corridors.

Masklin watched him go.

Not for the first time, he wished he believed in something as much as Gurder did so he could complain to it about his life. He even wished he were back, yes, back in the hole. It hadn't been too bad, apart from people being cold and wet and getting eaten all the time. But at least he'd been with Grimma. They would have been cold and wet and hungry together. He wouldn't have been so lonely. . . .

There was a movement by him. It turned out to be Pion, holding a tray of what had to be . . . fruit, Masklin decided. He put aside being lonely for a moment, and realized that hunger had been waiting for an opportunity to make itself felt. He'd never seen fruit that shape and color.

He took a slice from the proffered tray. It tasted like a nutty lemon.

"It's kept well, considering," he said, weakly. "Where did you get it?"

It turned out to come from a machine in a nearby corridor. It looked fairly simple. There were hundreds of pictures of different sorts of food. If you touched a picture, there was a brief humming noise and then the real food dropped onto a tray in a slot. Masklin tried pictures at random, and got several different sorts of fruit, a squeaky green vegetable thing, and a piece of meat that tasted rather like smoked salmon.

"I wonder how it does it?" he said aloud.

A voice from the wall beside him said: *"Would you understand if I told you about molecular breakdown and reassembly from a wide range of raw materials?"*

"No," said Masklin, truthfully.

"Then it's all done by Science."

"Oh. Well, that's all right, then. That *is* you, Thing, isn't it?"

"Yes."

Chewing on the fish-meat, Masklin wandered back to the control room and offered some of the food to Angalo. The big screen was showing nothing but clouds.

"Won't see any quarry in all this," he said.

Angalo pulled one of the levers back a bit. There was that brief feeling of extra weight again.

They stared at the screen.

"Wow," said Angalo.

"That looks familiar," said Masklin. He patted his clothes until he found the folded, crumpled map they'd brought all the way from the Store.

He spread it out, and glanced from it to the screen.

The screen showed a disc, made up mainly of different shades of blue and wispy bits of cloud.

"Any idea what it is?" said Angalo.

"No, but I know what some of the bits are called," said Masklin. "That one that's thick at the top and thin at the bottom is called South America. Look, it's just like it is on the map. Only it should have the words 'South America' written on it."

"Still can't see the quarry, though," said Angalo.

Masklin looked at the image in front of them. South America. Grimma had talked about South America, hadn't she? That's where the frogs lived in flowers. She'd said that once you knew about things like frogs living in flowers, you weren't the same person.

He was beginning to see what she meant.

"Never mind about the quarry for now," he said. "The quarry can wait."

"We should get there as soon as possible, for everybody's sake," said the Thing.

Masklin thought about this for a while. It was true, he had to admit. All kinds of things might be happening back home. He had to get the Ship back quickly, for everybody's sake.

And then he thought: I've spent a long time doing things for everybody's sake.

Just for once, I'm going to do something for me.

I don't think we can find other nomes with this Ship, but at least I know where to look for frogs.

"Thing," he said, "take us to South America—and don't argue."

Twelve

Frogs: Some people think that knowing about frogs is important. They are small and green, or yellow, and have four legs. They croak. Young frogs are tadpoles. In my opinion, this is all there is to know about frogs.

> —From *A Scientific Encyclopedia for the Enquiring Young Nome* by Angalo de Haberdasheri.

Find a blue planet. . . . *Focus.*

This is a planet. Most of it is covered with water, but it's still called Earth.

Find a country. . . . *Focus.* . . . Blues and greens and browns under the sun, and long wisps of rain cloud being torn by the mountains. . . . *Focus* . . . on a mountain, green and dripping, and there's a . . . *focus* . . . tree, hung with moss and covered with flowers, and . . . *focus* . . . on a flower with a little pool in it, is an epiphytic bromeliad.

Its leaves, although they might be petals, hardly quiver at all as three very small and very golden frogs pull themselves up and gaze in astonishment at the fresh, clear water. Two of them look at their leader, waiting for it to say something suitable for this historic occasion.

It's going to say . . . *mipmip.* . . .

And then they slide down the leaf and into the water.

Although the frogs can spot the difference between day and night, they're a bit hazy on the whole idea of time. They know that some things happen after other things. Really intelligent frogs might wonder if there is something that prevents everything happening all at once, but that's about as close as they can get to it.

So how long it was before a strange night came in the middle of the day is hard to tell, from a frog point of view.

A wide black shadow drifted over the treetops, and came to a halt. After a while there were voices. The frogs could hear them, although they didn't know what they meant or even what they were. They didn't sound like the kind of voices frogs were used to.

What they heard went like this:

"How many mountains are there, anyway? I mean, it's ridiculous! Who needs this many mountains? I call it inefficient. One would have done.

I'll go mad if I see another mountain. How many more have we got to search?"

"I like them."

"And some of the trees are the wrong height."

"I like them, too, Gurder."

"And I don't trust Angalo doing the driving."

"I think he's getting better, Gurder."

"Well, I just hope no more airplanes come flying around, that's all."

Gurder and Masklin swung in a crude basket made out of bits of metal and wire. It hung from a square hatchway under the Ship.

There were still huge rooms in the Ship that they hadn't explored yet. Odd machines were everywhere. The Thing had said the Ship had been used for exploring.

Masklin hadn't quite trusted any of it. There probably were machines that could have lowered and pulled up the basket easily, but he'd preferred to loop the wire around a pillar inside the Ship, and with Pion helping inside, to pull themselves up and down by sheer nomish effort.

The basket bumped gently on the tree branch.

The trouble was that humans wouldn't leave them alone. No sooner had they found a likely looking mountain than airplanes or helicopters would buzz around, like insects around an eagle. It was distracting.

Masklin looked along the branch. Gurder was right. This would have to be the last mountain.

But there certainly were flowers here.

He crawled along the branch until he reached the nearest flower. It was three times as high as he was. He found a foothold and pulled himself up.

There was a pool in there. Six little yellow eyes peered up at him.

Masklin stared back.

So it was true, after all.

He wondered if there was anything he should say to them, if there was anything they could possibly understand.

It was quite a long branch, and quite thick. But there were tools and things in the Ship. They could let down extra wires to hold the branch and winch it up when it was cut free. It would take some time, but that didn't matter. It was important.

The Thing had said there were ways of growing plants under lights the same color as the sun, in pots full of a sort of weak soup that helped plants grow. It should be the easiest thing to keep a branch alive. The easiest thing in the world.

If they did everything carefully and gently, the frogs would never know.

If the world was a bathtub, the progress of the Ship through it would be like the soap, shooting backward and forward and never being where anyone expected it to be. You could spot where it had just been by airplanes and helicopters taking off in a hurry.

Or maybe it was like the ball in a roulette wheel, bouncing around and looking for the right number.

Or maybe it was just lost.

They searched all night. If there was a night. It was hard to tell. The Thing tried to explain that the Ship went faster than the sun, although the sun actually stood still. Some parts of the world had night while other parts had day. This, Gurder said, was bad organization.

"In the Store," he said, "it was always dark when it should be. Even if it *was* just somewhere built by humans." It was the first time they'd heard him admit the Store was built by humans.

There didn't seem to be anywhere that looked familiar.

Masklin scratched his chin.

"The Store was in a place called Blackbury," he said. "I know that much. So the quarry couldn't have been far away."

Angalo waved his hand irritably at the screens.

"Yes, but it's not like the map," he said. "They don't stick names on places! It's ridiculous! How's anyone supposed to know where anywhere is?"

"All right," said Masklin. "But you're *not* to fly down low again to try to read the signposts. Every time you do that, humans rush out into the streets and we get lots of shouting on the radio."

"That's right," said the Thing. *"People are bound to get excited when they see a ten-million-ton starship trying to fly down the street."*

"I was very careful last time," said Angalo stoutly. "I even stopped when the traffic lights went red. I don't see why there was such a fuss. All the trucks and cars started crashing into one another too. And you call *me* a bad driver."

Gurder turned to Pion, who was learning the language fast. The geese nomes did. They were used to meeting nomes who spoke other languages.

"Your geese never got lost," he said. "How did they manage it?"

"They just did not get lost," said Pion. "They knew always where they going."

"It can be like that with animals," said Masklin. "They've got instincts. It's like knowing things without knowing you know them."

"I don't know," said Gurder. "Why doesn't the Thing know? It could find Floridia, so somewhere important like Blackbury ought to be *no* trouble."

"I can find no radio messages about Blackbury. There are plenty about Florida," said the Thing.

"At least land *somewhere*," said Gurder. Angalo pressed a couple of buttons.

"There's just sea under us right now," he said. "And—what's that?"

Below the Ship and a long way off, something tiny and white skimmed over the clouds.

"Could be goose," said Pion.

"I . . . don't . . . think . . . so," said Angalo carefully. He twiddled a knob. "I'm really learning about this stuff," he said.

The picture of the screen flickered a bit, and then expanded.

There was a white dart sliding across the sky.

"Is it the Concorde?" said Gurder.

"Yes," said Angalo.

"It's going a bit slow, isn't it?"

"Only compared to us," said Angalo.

"Follow it," said Masklin.

"We don't know where it's going," said Angalo, in a reasonable tone of voice.

"I do," said Masklin. "You looked out the window when we were on the Concorde. We were going toward the sun."

"Yes. It was setting," said Angalo. "Well?"

"It's morning now. It's going toward the sun again," Masklin pointed out.

"Well? What about it?"

"It means it's going home."

Angalo bit his lip while he worked this out.

"I don't see why the sun has to rise and set in different places," said Gurder, who refused even to try to understand basic astronomy.

"Going home," said Angalo, ignoring him. "Right. I see it. So we go with it, yes?"

"Yes."

Angalo ran his hands over the Ship's controls.

"Right," he said. "Here we go. I expect the Concorde drivers will probably be quite pleased to have some company up here."

The Ship drew level with the plane.

"It's moving around a lot," said Angalo. "And it's starting to go faster too."

"I think they may be worried about the Ship," said Masklin.

"Can't see why," said Angalo. "Can't see why at all. We're not doing anything except following them."

"I wish we had some proper windows," said Gurder, wistfully. "We could wave."

"Have humans ever seen a Ship like this before?" Angalo asked the Thing.

"No. But they've made up stories about ships coming from other worlds."

"Yes, they'd do that," said Masklin, half to himself. "That's *just* the sort of thing they'd do."

"Sometimes they say the ships will contain friendly people—"

"That's us," said Angalo.

"And sometimes they say they will contain monsters with wavy tentacles and big teeth."

The nomes looked at one another.

Gurder cast an apprehensive eye over his shoulder.

Then they all stared at the passages that radiated off the control room.

"Like alligators?" said Masklin.

"*Worse.*"

"Er," Gurder said, "We *did* look in all the rooms, didn't we?"

"It's something they made up, Gurder. It's not real," said Masklin.

"Whoever would want to make up something like that?"

"Humans would," said Masklin.

"Huh," said Angalo, nonchalantly trying to swivel around in the chair in case any tentacled things with teeth were trying to creep up on him. "I can't see why."

"I think I can. I've been thinking about humans a lot."

"Can't the Thing send a message to the Concorde drivers?" said Gurder. "Something like 'Don't worry, we haven't got any teeth and tentacles, guaranteed'?"

"They probably wouldn't believe us," said Angalo. "If *I* had teeth and tentacles all over the place that's just the sort of message I'd send. Cunning."

The Concorde screamed across the top of the sky, breaking the transatlantic record. The Ship drifted along behind it.

"I reckon," said Angalo, looking down, "that humans are just about intelligent enough to be crazy."

"I think," said Masklin, "that maybe they're intelligent enough to be lonely."

The plane touched down with its tires screaming. Fire engines raced across the airport, and there were other vehicles behind them.

The great black ship shot over them, turned across the sky like a Frisbee, and slowed.

"There's the reservoir!" said Gurder. "Right under us! And that's the railway line! And that's the quarry! It's still there!"

"Of course it's still there, idiot," muttered Angalo as he headed the Ship toward the hills, which were patchy with melting snow.

"Some of it," said Masklin.

A pall of black smoke hung over the quarry. As they got closer, they saw it was rising from a burning truck. There were more trucks around it, and also several humans, who started to run when they saw the shadow of the Ship.

"Lonely, eh?" snarled Angalo. "If they've hurt a single nome, they'll wish they'd never been born!"

"If they've hurt a single nome, they'll wish *I'd* never been born," said Masklin. "But I don't think anyone's down there. They wouldn't hang around if the humans came. And who set fire to the truck?"

"Yay!" said Angalo, waving a fist in the air.

Masklin scanned the landscape below them. Somehow he couldn't imagine people like

Grimma and Dorcas sitting in holes, waiting for humans to take over. Trucks didn't just set fire to themselves. A couple of buildings looked damaged too. Humans wouldn't have done that, would they?

He stared at the field by the quarry. The gate had been smashed, and a pair of wide tracks led through the slush and mud.

"I think they got away in another truck," he said.

"What do you mean, *yay*?" said Gurder, lagging a bit behind the conversation.

"Across the fields?" said Angalo. "It'd get stuck, wouldn't it?"

Masklin shook his head. Perhaps even a nome could have instincts. "Follow the tracks," he said urgently. "And quickly!"

"Quickly? *Quickly?* Do you know how difficult it is to make this thing go *slow*?" Angalo nudged a lever. The Ship lurched up the hillside, straining at the indignity of restraint.

They'd been up here before, on foot, months ago. It was hard to believe.

The hills were quite flat on the top, forming a kind of plateau overlooking the airport. There was the field where there had been potatoes. There was the thicket where they'd hunted, and the wood where they'd killed a fox for eating nomes.

And there . . . there was something small and yellow, rolling across the fields.

Angalo craned forward.

"Looks like some kind of a machine," he admitted, fumbling for levers without taking his eyes off the screen. "Weird kind of one, though."

There were other things moving on the roads down there. They had flashing lights on top.

"Those cars are chasing it, do you think?" said Angalo.

"Maybe they want to talk to it about a burning truck," said Masklin. "Can you get to it before they do?"

Angalo narrowed his eyes. "Listen, I think we can get to it before they do even if we go via Floridia." He found another lever and gave it a nudge.

There was the briefest flicker in the landscape, and the truck was now right in front of them.

"See?" he said.

"Move in more," said Masklin.

Angalo pressed a button.

"See, the screen can show you below—" he began.

"There's nomes!" said Gurder.

"Yeah, and those cars are running away!" shouted Angalo. "That's it, run away! Otherwise it's teeth and tentacles time!"

"So long as the nomes don't think that too," said Gurder. "Masklin, do you think—"

Once again, Masklin wasn't there.

* * *

I should have thought about this before, he thought.

The piece of branch was thirty times longer than a nome. They'd been keeping it under lights, and it seemed to be growing quite happily with one end in a pot of special plant water. The nomes who had once flown in the Ship had grown lots of plants that way.

Pion helped him drag the pot toward the hatch. The frogs watched Masklin with interest.

When it was positioned as well as the two of them could manage, Masklin let the hatch open. It wasn't one that slid aside. The ancient nomes had used it as some kind of elevator, but it didn't have wires—it went up and down by some force as mysterious as auntie's gravy or whatever that was.

It dropped away. Masklin looked down and saw the yellow truck roll to a halt.

When he straightened up, Pion was giving him a puzzled look.

"Flower is a message?" said the boy.

"Yes. Kind of."

"Not using words?"

"No," said Masklin.

"Why not?"

Masklin shrugged.

"Don't know how to say them."

It nearly ends there. . . .
But it shouldn't end there.

* * *

Nomes swarmed all over the Ship. If there *were* any monsters with tentacles and teeth, they'd have been overwhelmed by sheer force of nome.

Young nomes filled the control room, where they were industriously trying to press buttons. Dorcas and his trainee engineers had disappeared in search of the Ship's engines. Voices and laughter echoed along the gray corridors.

Masklin and Grimma sat by themselves, watching the frogs in their flower.

"I had to see if it was true," said Masklin.

"The most wonderful thing in the world," said Grimma. "You know, a bromeliad looks quite different from what I expected."

"No. I think there are probably much more wonderful things in the world," said Masklin. "But it's pretty good, all the same."

Grimma told him about events in the quarry, the fight with the humans, and the stealing of the Cat to escape. Her eyes gleamed when she talked about fighting humans. Masklin looked at her with his mouth open in admiration. She was muddy, her dress was torn, her hair looked like it had been combed with a hedge, but she crackled with so much internal energy that she nearly was throwing off sparks. It's a good thing we got here in time, he thought. Humans ought to thank me.

"What are we going to do now?" she said.

"I don't know," said Masklin. "Try to find

home, I suppose. Or *a* home. According to the
Thing, there's lots of worlds out there with nomes
on them. Just nomes, I mean. Or we can find one
all to ourselves. A *new* home. That might be even
better."

"You know," said Grimma, "I think the Store
nomes would be happier just staying on the Ship.
That's why they like it so much. It's like being in
the Store. All the Outside is outside."

"Then I'd better go along to make sure they remember that there *is* an Outside. It's sort of my
job, I suppose," said Masklin. "And, when we've
found somewhere, I want to bring the Ship back."

"Why? What'll be here?" said Grimma.

"Other nomes."

"Oh, yes," said Grimma.

"And humans," said Masklin. "We should talk
to them."

"What?"

"They really want to believe in . . . I mean,
they spend all their time making up stories about
things that don't exist. They think it's just themselves in the world. We never thought like that. We
always *knew* there were humans. They're terribly
lonely and don't know it." He waved his hands
vaguely. "It's just that I think we might get along
with them," he finished.

"They'd turn us into pixies!"

"Not if we come back in the Ship. If there's one

thing even humans can tell, it's that the Ship isn't very pixieish."

Grimma reached out and took his hand.

"Well . . . if that's what you really want to do."

"It is."

"I'll come back with you."

There was a sound behind them. It was Gurder. The Abbot had a bag slung around his neck and had the drawn, determined look of someone who is going to See It Through no matter what.

"Er. I've come to say good-bye," he said.

"What do you mean?" said Masklin.

"I heard you say you're coming back in the Ship?"

"Yes, but—"

"Please don't argue." Gurder looked around. "I've been thinking about this ever since we got on the Ship. There *are* other nomes out there. *Someone* ought to tell them about the Ship coming back. We can't take them now, but someone ought to find all the other nomes in the world and make sure that they know about the Ship. Someone ought to be telling them about what's really true. It should be me, don't you think? I've got to be useful for *something*."

"All by *yourself*?" said Masklin.

Gurder rummaged in the bag.

"No, I'm taking the Thing," he said, producing the black cube.

"Er—" Masklin began.

"Don't worry," said the Thing. *"I have copied myself into the Ship's own computers. I can be here and there at the same time."*

"It's something I really want to do," said Gurder helplessly.

Masklin thought about arguing and then thought, Why? Gurder will probably be happier like this. Anyway, it's true. This Ship belongs to all nomes. We're just borrowing it for a while. So Gurder's right. Someone's got to find the rest of them, wherever they are in the world, and tell them the truth about nomes. I can't think of anyone better for the job than Gurder. It's a big world. You need someone really ready to believe really *hard*.

"Do you want anyone to go with you?" he said.

"No. I expect I'll find some nomes out there to help me. I've been talking to Pion." He leaned closer. "To tell the truth," he said, "I'm looking forward to it."

"Er. Yes. There's a lot of world, though," said Masklin. "You can't be sure you'll find any help."

"I'll have to hope, then."

"Well . . . if you're *sure* . . ." said Masklin doubtfully.

"Yes. More sure than anything I can remember," said Gurder. "And I've been pretty sure of a lot of things in my time, as you know."

"We'd better find somewhere suitable to set you down," said Masklin.

"That's right," said Gurder. He tried to look brave. "Somewhere with a lot of geese," he said.

They left him at sunset, by a lake.

It was a brief parting. If the Ship stayed anywhere for more than a few minutes now, humans would flock toward it.

"You were wrong to let him go," said Grimma as they closed the hatch. "He doesn't even know how to steer a goose!"

"I told him that, and he said that Pion gave him a few hints and if he couldn't find any goose nomes, then he'd learn himself," said Masklin. "He said that if the Floridians could do it, then he could too. He was very definite about it."

"He'd learn? Gurder? Just like that?" said Grimma.

"Well, you learned how to drive the Cat," said Masklin.

"Huh! That was different. I *had* to."

"Maybe there are things he has to do too. He's got a chance. Why should we try to stop him?"

"But we're his friends!"

"That's what I mean," said Masklin.

The last they saw of Gurder was a small, waving figure on the shore. And then there was just a lake turning into a green dot on a dwindling landscape. A world unfolded, with one invisible nome in the middle of it.

And then there was nothing.

The control room was full of nomes watching the landscape unroll as the Ship rose.

Grimma stared at it.

"I never realized it looked like that," said Grimma. "There's so much of it!"

"It's pretty big," said Masklin.

"You'd think one world would be big enough for all of us," said Grimma.

"Oh, I don't know," said Masklin. "Maybe one world isn't big enough for anyone. Where are we heading, Angalo?"

Angalo rubbed his hands and pulled every lever right back.

"So far up," he said, with satisfaction, "that there is no down."

The Ship curved away, toward the stars.

Below, the world stopped unrolling because it had reached its edges, and became a black disc against the sun.

Nomes and frogs looked down on it.

And the sunlight caught it and made it glow around the rim, sending rays up into the darkness, so that it looked exactly like a flower.

About the Author

TERRY PRATCHETT is the author of the immensely satisfying group of Discworld novels, which includes *Mort, Wyrd Sisters,* and *Equal Rites.* Although these books were intended for adults, they have a devoted following among younger readers as well. He is also coauthor of the highly acclaimed fantasy novel *Good Omens.*

Wings is the last volume in the Bromeliad Trilogy for young adults, following *Truckers* and *Diggers.* It concludes the career of the nomes on earth and gives them the whole universe—which maybe should be warned about nomes. . . .

Terry Pratchett's body lives in England. It says that the whereabouts of his mind is probably not locatable in any normal atlas.